He liked to dri... blood of his victims!

The Blood Doctor led his troops in a ruthless sweep of the desert village.

The natives were raped, beaten, brutally murdered by decapitation.

The Blood Doctor had prescribed carnage to quench his inhuman thirst. Slaughter was his sport.

When the village was totally ravaged, he moved on, eager to make his mark on the world—in scars.

Government forces were unable to stop the destruction by the rampaging killers. Under the hellish desert sun, Mack Bolan's Phoenix Force roared into action. Their target—the Blood Doctor!

Mack Bolan's
PHOENIX FORCE

Mack Bolan's
ABLE TEAM

MACK BOLAN
The Executioner

PHOENIX FORCE

AN EXECUTIONER SERIES

Aswan Hellbox

Gar Wilson

A GOLD EAGLE BOOK FROM
WORLDWIDE

TORONTO · NEW YORK · LONDON · PARIS
AMSTERDAM · STOCKHOLM · HAMBURG
ATHENS · MILAN · TOKYO · SYDNEY

First edition November 1983

ISBN 0-373-61308-3

Special thanks and acknowledgment to
Thomas P. Ramirez and Sergeant Rex Swenson
for their contributions to this work.

Printed in Canada

1

The Black Cobras, two hundred eighty men strong, came upon the woebegone village of Abu Darash at roughly 0900 hours. They were hungry, weary, thirsty. And mean.

On the run since shortly after midnight, fleeing the scene of a firefight just inside the Chad border—where they had left behind at least forty dead—they were in no mood for the usual amenities. Vicious and surly, they would casually cut down anyone who so much as crossed their path.

Already the blazing April sun was turning the desert into a blistering hell. The sky was shimmering, suggesting far-off rivers, lakes, oceans stretching in everlasting taunt where absolutely no water existed. The searing wind, the heat—temperatures would easily reach one hundred ten degrees by midafternoon—the mirages' empty promise infuriated the sullen black mercenaries, darkening their mood to a dangerous flashpoint.

All this was to the misfortune of the hundred twenty-two inhabitants of Abu Darash.

Most of the village's men and boys were in the fields, tending to what grains grew in the desert; or they were driving goat herds to sparse vegetation. Only the old men, women and children remained behind to face the initial wrath of General Jeremiah Blackwell and the scum composing his army.

The troops had been seen a long way off, their military convoy throwing up high clouds of dust on the horizon. When the first dozen of the Unimog armored trucks came into view, the villagers remained more curious than frightened. After all, Abu Darash was isolated, at the end of the world. Nothing ever happened here.

But as the armored Land Rover swept around the convoy's right flank, screeched to a stop in the village's main square, the villagers became nervous. Naked children scuttled back inside the primitive stick-and-mud huts or cowered behind their mothers' long skirts. Some of the women slowly edged back, becoming lost in the maze of rude fences.

It was *the man* himself who struck the most jarring note. A tall, thin black man, dressed entirely in black, a gaudy dress cap jauntily placed atop his head, he stood stiff as a ramrod in his staff car, his eyes coldly surveying the villagers lining the street. There was a psychotic emptiness in his eyes, a hint of cruelty in his contemptuous half smile that immediately chilled those villagers perceptive enough to sniff trouble before it happened.

The men who sat aboard the Unimog personnel carriers—a dozen khaki-uniformed soldiers to a truck—were armed to the teeth, festooned with bandoliers, cartridge cases, each sporting a new Kalashnikov AK-47 assault rifle. They regarded the Kababish tribesmen with matching contempt, a sadistic anticipation glowing dully in their eyes.

Little by little more vehicles drew into Abu Darash, among them ten-ton trucks loaded with more troops. An odd-lot assortment of command cars, even a vintage German half-track, continued to wedge themselves into the cramped opening. These transported Blackwell's officer cadre, subordinates who were apparently eager to be as near to their leader as possible. Their expressions were full of rapt, mesmerized adoration for the hard-faced American—Africa's self-proclaimed new savior.

It was imperative to Blackwell that Major Chilufia Ochogilo, the Black Cobra's second-in-command, be close by. Though Blackwell had learned to speak a bastardized version of the Arabic dialect spoken in north Sudan, his vocabulary was limited. Once his opening greetings were delivered he generally lapsed into English. It was Ochogilo's place to translate.

But today there would be no sales pitch. "Where are your men?" Blackwell bullied them once the hubbub in the square died down. "Have the cowardly dogs gone to hide from the Blood Doctor?"

Though his Arabic was halting and faulty, his message was glaringly clear. The citizens of Abu Darash were immediately filled with terror. Slavers had long been a part of the Kababish heritage. And now the slavers were back.

The women, fear etched on their faces, began to mutter and wail among themselves.

"They are in the fields," a frightened female replied. "At work on the *feddan*s." Her hand pointed east.

It was all Blackwell's thugs needed. Immediately

orders were barked. Three Unimogs, a Goryonov SG34 medium machine gun mounted on each, peeled off and headed toward the fields. An unmarked gray-and-tan truck, its canopy stiff with dust, was swiftly emptied, sent to carry back the conscripts.

A few women and some of the old men made moves to escape, to run and warn their menfolk. But their decision came too late, and they quickly found themselves ringed by Black Cobra mercenaries. The AK-47s came up menacingly, and the women froze, waiting for what would come next. Terror twisted their faces as they read the hot, lustful glitter in the soldiers' eyes. Some began to weep, others pleaded to be spared.

While Blackwell waited for his thugs to return, there was time to attend to other needs. With more than seven hundred fifty miles of basically unplotted desert before them, oases and villages few and far between. . . .

"Water," the boss man commanded. "Tell my men where the water is. We have come a long way, and our tanks are empty." Turning to Major Ochogilo, he said, "Get every reserve tank, every canteen filled. We have no idea when we'll find a well again."

The demand was almost worse than the dire threat already facing Abu Darash. The government had recently supplied them with a donkey-engine pump to bring up precious water from the village well, but they were nearing the end of the Dar Kababish dry season; the water level was precariously low. To share with greedy outsiders would be disastrous.

The women set up even louder protest, begging the invaders to go on without their water.

Ochogilo flung a torrent of Arabic orders at his underlings. They seized a white-bearded male and pulled him from the throng. One looping swing of a Kalashnikov butt and the old man was rolling on the hardscrabble road, his face gushing blood. "You will lead my men to the well," Blackwell's flunky stormed. "Any further delay and you die."

The man struggled to his feet and began staggering toward the far end of the village, a rifle-wielding merc close on his heels. Unimog engines growled; one by one they wheeled, headed down the road and formed a line, waiting their turn at the pump. The men cursed the building heat, sweat streaming down their faces as they sat in the blast-furnace sun. The sluggard pump only brought up a quart a minute, it seemed.

Tempers grew shorter by the minute. A half hour later, when the transport bearing the forty-odd men of the village arrived, the terrorist force was verging on mutiny.

Had they not earlier been challenged by the hot-headed Front for Chadian Liberation as they had emerged from their rocky Chad staging area near Djirkjik, had they not had their butts royally kicked by the wily, Tuareg-infested force, things might have been different.

The bloody defeat had become a grim omen. No way to begin a mission. Small wonder morale was at low ebb.

But, Blackwell mused, when one must deal with snarling dogs, throw them raw meat.

In his eyes, the women of Abu Darash were, for the most part, as ugly as a hatful of warts. But when young men have been in bivouac for nearly a month....

The village women would do. They would do very nicely.

Everything in due course, he concluded, letting his eyes slide over the females, taking a decided fancy to a young, lithe-bodied woman off to the right. Wearing a fresh blue *taub*, an enameled medallion in her right nostril, she was without a doubt the most beautiful in the village. Barely twenty, her skin a glowing coffee color, she was unmistakably virgin. Unveiled (as was the custom in this part of Sudan), disdaining any head covering, her lustrous black hair fell halfway down her back and was very appealing to Blackwell.

At that moment the female looked up at him, apprehension in her eyes, and the Black Cobra leader knew a great need. As their eyes locked, the girl dropped her gaze, furtively attempted to fade into the crowd.

"That woman there," he snapped to Major Ochogilo, "she's mine, Chilufia. No other man touches her, understand?"

The major smiled. "Of course, General," he replied in a nasal, rasping version of English. "You have decided then? To let the troops have their sport?"

Blackwell swallowed a smile of his own. "When it's time." He nodded in the beauty's direction again. "Orders, Major," he reminded.

"Yes, sir," the fat, perspiring man dressed in soiled khakis responded. Immediately he dispatched two men to collect the girl. He felt twinges of his own as he saw the troops pull her from the clutch of wailing matrons. The young woman fought like a wildcat.

Judging from past performances Ochogilo had witnessed, Blackwell had a particularly cruel, dominating way with his women. Perhaps, as had happened in the past, his boss would allow him to have seconds.

He nodded his approval as the soldiers dragged the screaming woman to his command car and pushed her roughly into the back seat. The other women set up an unholy chorus of sobs, but the Black Cobra regulars closed ranks, brandished their rifles, threatened them with similar treatment. The females quickly lost some of their fire.

All except for one female, the captured woman's mother, who kept trying to break through the cordon. An impatient trooper finally clubbed her on the side of the head with his fist. She sank to the ground with a moan, shook her head groggily, then let her neighbors draw her back inside the human corral.

Abruptly Jeremiah Blackwell became all business. They had country to cover—this stopover was consuming too much time. As the men of Abu Darash were roughly pushed from the back of the ten-ton truck and herded into an opening to the left of the women's place of confinement, Blackwell emerged from the Land Rover, paced wordlessly before them, his eyes hard, his finger darting. Each time he pointed, Black Cobra troops dragged a man aside and flung him into a separate line.

When thirty of the most rugged, ablebodied specimens were chosen, Blackwell ceased his prowling. Standing with his hands folded behind his back, he rocked on his heels and commenced his recruitment spiel.

There was time—there was always time—for a quick outline of his program for Africa. In essence: Africa for the black. He would not rest in his holy crusade until the last white man had been killed or driven from its shores.

The Black Cobras had lost many men in their last battle with the African oppressors, he told them. He needed dedicated men to replace the heroes who had so recently given their lives for the cause. Again he paced with dramatic slowness, regarded the candidates squarely. Were there any volunteers?

The reluctant prospects exchanged pained smiles, looked off into space. Still not appreciating the gravity of their situation, they thought to stonewall the whole thing. Just ignore the raving lunatic. He would go away and leave them alone.

But it was not that simple. And Blackwell—a strutting, paratroop-booted Napoleon with a Colt automatic strapped to his hip—smiled coldly, recognizing the need to capture the attention of these shuffling rustics. To this purpose he approached one of the lesser specimens, a Juba black, whose face was grotesquely scarred from a boyhood tsetse infection, one eyelid swollen permanently shut.

"Do you volunteer?" he boomed in his best Arabic, his tone friendly yet menacing at the same time. "Will you accept the honor of being the first man from Abu Darash to join the Black Cobras?"

The man, perhaps twenty-five, shrugged, smiled foolishly, but said nothing.

"I offer you a second chance," Blackwell said, his voice louder, cold fury barely suppressed. A strange, ominous silence closed in on the square. *"Do you volunteer?"*

The pitiful peasant, truly out of his depth, actually giggled. "No, effendi," he replied apologetically, hoping that politeness would suffice.

There was no warning. Moving with incredible speed, using a hip slap that had taken endless hours to perfect, he whipped the Colt .45 out of its holster, aimed and fired in one sweep. The automatic boomed once, the .45 slug blowing away the poor villager's nose, emerging from the back of his head with a volcanic gush of blood, gray matter and bone that splashed the astonished man behind him full in the face.

The farmer swayed on his feet and turned a slow half circle. His face registering bloody dismay, he staggered backward, forward, then made a move to fall.

Two of Blackwell's hardmen moved in and caught the man. Even as he was braced in a forty-five-degree incline, another man, carrying a gleaming silver bowl, hurried forward. Placing the pint container directly beneath the gaping wound, he collected the victim's blood until the bowl was half full.

A keening sigh went over the compound as the bowl was handed to Blackwell. Pausing for effect, his eyes defiantly sweeping the crowd, he lifted the bowl to his lips. With slow, savoring gulps he drank the hot blood, held the bowl at extreme cant to receive every last drop.

The unconsulted blood donor had been unceremoniously dropped to the ground, his blood forming a puddle in the sand. Already the hole in the back of his head was aswarm with hundreds of snarling flies.

Blackwell handed the empty bowl to a hardguy and turned toward the soldiers-to-be. They were struck dumb. It was high drama, exceedingly effective, touching raw nerves, exciting an ageless superstition and fear of the supernatural. Black Cobra troops fell to their knees, prostrated themselves.

Even though the ritual was now routine to them, most were still chilled, their belief in their headman's spooky omnipotence again reinforced. *"Blood Doctor,"* they began to chant. *"Blood Doctor, Blood Doctor...."*

If the villagers had known terror before, then this new charade was beyond terror. They commenced falling to their knees, as well.

The chant built up. *"Blood Doctor...."*

But to some of the conscripts, the prospect of serving such a demonic master was altogether too frightening. Some tried to escape.

There was sudden outcry to the left as eight of the bolder men surged forward, tried to batter their way through Black Cobra lines. But their efforts were for nought. The brainwashed hardmen were anticipating such a breakout.

Rifle butts slashed and thudded viciously; the would-be runaways were stopped cold.

If something had snapped within the brains of these panicky conscripts, it was nothing compared to the explosion of psychotic outrage that their defiance ignited in Jeremiah Blackwell's brain. In that moment he came unglued.

"Bring those yellow bastards up here," he roared in English. *"Now."* Major Ochogilo instantly repeated the commands in Arabic. "They dare to reject the Blood Doctor?" His eyes flashed with a maniacal glitter. "They must pay."

Each of the disobedient men was clubbed forward, thrown to his hands and knees before Blackwell. Though they struggled like madmen, they were no match for the Black Cobra troops. Then, as Blackwell approached, the guards went stiff, already wincing against the close-range thunder that would shortly jar their eardrums.

Blackwell's stride was rapid as he went from victim to victim. The coup de grace was swift, the .45 snugged tight to the base of the first five men's skulls. The automatic blasted, flinging each man to the ground.

With each shot, Blackwell's paranoia soared. He signaled that the other three rebels should be dragged toward a distant acacia stump that stood beside one of the mud-walled huts. The poor men began to scream and plead desperately as they saw the long, razor-sharp *panga* brought from Blackwell's Land Rover. And as the madman's stooges stretched the fingers of each man's left hand over the stump and held it fast, Blackwell raised the fearsome machete high over his head. The men screamed even more hideously. Even if they should survive the insane mutilation, it was still the most horrendous humiliation that could be inflicted upon a Muslim. In days ahead the missing left hand would render him an untouchable; he would be forever marked as a thief.

Blackwell knew full well what he was doing. He had long steeped himself in African culture; he knew how to hit these people where they lived. He actually laughed as he saw the men flopping on the ground, one jumping up, running around the compound like a spinning dervish, blood spurting from the stump in torrents.

More than likely all three would die from loss of blood, infection or worse. He did not care. It was the message he sought to convey to the other men, to those few villagers who might survive, that mattered. The Blood Doctor—so the legend would spread—was not a man to be taken lightly.

Yes, Blackwell understood the population's psychology well.

Blackwell strode to where the main group of men stood in rubber-kneed shock, abject fear glistening in their eyes. Arms akimbo, the bloody machete held in his right hand, he regarded them coldly. Then, in a threatening voice he said, "Do I have volunteers now?"

"*Aywa*, effendi." They almost fell over themselves to respond en masse. "*Aywa, aywa....*" Yes. A million yeses.

"Pick out some others," Blackwell ordered Major Ochogilo, "to make up for the ones I disciplined. Get them into number-three truck. Put your toughest guards on them. They might get riled when we start messing with the women."

"Yes, General," Ochogilo replied, an ugly leer forming on his face. He barked rapid-fire commands to a select, hard-core cadre. Prodding the recruits with their rifles, they drove them toward the trucks like cattle. The guards vented their resentment upon the Kababish tribesmen because they were certain they would miss out on the fun once the Blood Doctor declared open season on the women.

Blackwell strode arrogantly toward the seventy-odd women, children and old men. The Black Cobra guards parted respectfully, giving him access to the core of the jabbering throng. The females recoiled as he approached, frantic to escape the contaminating touch of this Satan personified. Revulsion, hatred, fear distorted their features.

"You," Blackwell growled, singling out a tall, angular female of about thirty, who was dressed in a dirty white *taub*, "come over here."

The woman moaned, cringed, tried to ease back into the crowd. "Please, please, effendi," she babbled. "Spare me. I have done nothing wrong."

"Come here," he repeated. "Do you remember what happens to people who refuse to do my bidding? Come here, I said."

Finally the scar-faced female forced herself forward, torn between conflicting fears. When she faltered, her fearful sisters, hoping that she would be suitable sacrifice, that they would be spared, nudged her forward. She stood before her new master in slumped dejection.

"My boots, hag," he said. "Don't you see they are covered with blood? Don't just stand there. Clean them."

The woman looked about confusedly. Clean this demon's boots? But how? With what?

"Your robe, bitch," Blackwell snapped. "It will do nicely. Move."

But as the woman sank to her knees and made a clumsy move to scrub away the gore on his shoes with the hem of her *taub*, Blackwell dug his fingers into the kline of the loosely draped garment. "Not like that," he spat, giving the robe a vicious pull. "Like this."

The woman clutched the *taub*, fought to keep her body covered, but her backward motion only helped drag the flimsy cotton away, and she sank in half-sitting position, her naked body totally exposed. A piteous sob escaping her lips, she fought to cover herself.

But now Blackwell's automatic was once more in full view, held menacingly to her head. "Take it off, slut," he rasped. "Are you too proud to clean my boots?"

His eyes bored into hers. Would she dare to refuse the humiliating demand? The woman's eyes were crazy. Then, with a muffled wail, she dropped the robe. Crawling closer, she began wiping the blood away with bunched folds of the gown.

There was swift intake of breath in the town square—by the women and children, by the Black Cobra troops themselves.

The mercenaries crowded even closer, each eager to have first chance at the available females. The ratio of women to men stood at one to six.

Blackwell's eyes slowly assessed the women of Abu Darash where they stood in paralyzed shock, all recognizing the hopelessness of their situation. "My men have been in the field a long time," he mocked. "They have been without women. They are much in need, as you can well imagine. Which of you will be the first to *volunteer* to satisfy this need?''

While at his feet, the dazed blubbering woman, moving like a robot, continued to polish his boots long after the last of the blood was gone.

''Ah, here we go,'' he said, his sick enjoyment of raw power absolute now. ''This one will do very nicely. She will be noble example to you all.'' With that he leaned down, dragged the protesting female to her feet. Quickly he pushed her toward the nearest soldier. ''Here, my friend,'' he chuckled, ''enjoy yourself.''

The soldier grinned broadly, clamped his fingers in her hair, began dragging her through the cordon of soldiers, some of whom peeled off and followed, eager to be second and third in line.

It was the signal they had been awaiting, and with a guttural roar, the rest of Blackwell's troops closed in and began dragging the screaming, sobbing women away from their enclave. The din was suddenly deafening, a cacophony of shrill outcry, of curses and threats, as soldiers fought to subdue their women or as they fought between themselves for a particular victim.

It seemed the cries and laughter and cursing went on for hours, when, in reality, it was a matter of thirty to forty minutes before the men had their fill, and the women lay in comatose collapse, many dead. In brotherly benevolence the troops even went to spell their comrades who guarded the truckload of recruits, pointed them toward the most presentable females.

Catalyst for the bloody conclusion of the day's action was provided by a crusty old man, who had managed to dig out an antique rifle from a secret cache. Thinking to protect some women, he received a dozen 7.62mm rounds in the gut for his heroic pains. The degenerate sport went on unhindered.

From there it was only one step to wholesale slaughter. A villager had actually dared to fire on one of their mates. The angered troops then ranged from hut to hut, firing madly, murdering any women, children or oldsters still alive. Out in the square the men deemed unfit for service with Blackwell's army had long since been dispatched; their bodies lay in bloody tangle in the sun, wounds alive with voracious flies.

General Jeremiah Blackwell, standing apart, watched with cold impassivity.

Had there been a moment's thought about possible retaliation for the atrocities from the Sudan authorities? Hardly. The government, the army were totally inept, corruption riddled. What happened in the hinterlands hardly mattered. Besides, Blackwell thought, *he* was the law. *He* was a power unto himself. He was destined to become even more powerful in Africa in the days ahead.

So, let the troops play. Let them indulge their most sadistic fantasies.

After the gunfire died down, he sent Captain Oyoo and his crew forth with their cans of black paint. They would leave defiant signs for all the world to see. When they were finished, the mark of the Black Cobra—a stylized hooded snake, tail coiled in readiness to strike—was emblazoned on the wall of each of Abu Darash's thirty-eight huts.

Should someone manage to survive this raid, they

would long remember the work of this day. They would remember the Black Cobras. They would remember General Jeremiah Blackwell.

Almost as an afterthought the psycho despot decreed a final grisly memorial to his visit. The bodies of two women and a twelve-year-old girl were dragged from a hut. Timbers from a community house—smooth pickets about eight feet long—were sharpened to extreme point.

As the twenty-vehicle convoy pulled out at 1130 hours, Blackwell smiled back approvingly at the way his men had buried the poles in the ground, at the primitive way the three females had been impaled, each on her own picket.

Waving back to Major Ochogilo, catching sight of the dusky beauty who had been reserved for his private purposes, he had cause to grin more broadly. Perhaps he would enjoy her tonight. Tomorrow night? He could be a patient man at times.

Now, as the three totems gradually became smaller, faded into the everlasting sameness of the desert, he heaved a long, contented sigh.

A good day's work, he concluded.

2

The men of Phoenix Force arrived at what remained of Abu Darash about forty-eight hours after the massacre. Thrown off course by a ten-hour sandstorm, they had lost precious time trying to get a new fix on Blackwell's line of march. By the time they had come upon the site of the firefight between Blackwell's army and the intransigent troops of the Front for Chadian Liberation and had assessed the Black Cobra losses of men and equipment, another day had been wasted.

Now they were at least two days behind his batallions.

Blackwell's tracks had been lost again and again in the drifting, parching sands of the Libyan desert. In the end, relying on instinct, on compass readings, knowing from Hal Brognola's stateside briefings that their quarry was headed in a general east northeast direction, they blindly consigned themselves to the tender mercies of Lady Luck.

And this scorching April morning at 1100 hours....

"Dear God in heaven," Gary Manning said as they came within sight of the desolate village, and the smell of rotting flesh swept out to meet them. "What the hell has gone on here?"

It was then, as Manning topped a minor rise, and

they had an overview of the burned-out cluster of huts, that the three impaled bodies—bloated, glistening in the sun—came into clear view. Also in sickening view were bloated and festering bodies scattered everywhere in the village streets.

"Oh, bloody hell," McCarter groaned. Behind them, in the fast attack vehicle—FAV, which was in tow, Keio Ohara leaned over the side, verging on upchuck.

Each member of the team cringed and was seemingly diminished somehow by the blatant display of man's basic inhumanity to man.

"It's that slime Blackwell," McCarter said. "He's been here, sure as hell."

Even in the hundred-five-degree heat each man was scourged by a fleeting splash of goose bumps. The man responsible for this atrocity, they reasoned, was the same man they had been sent to Africa to wipe out. What kind of a fiend, what kind of an adversary did they face?

"Hey." Encizo broke the silence when his stomach had finally stopped going round and round. "I don't need this. Let's give it a pass."

"No," their grim-faced Israeli headman replied. "There might be survivors. We have to check. It's the least we can do." He touched Manning's shoulder. "Let's go down."

They parked within a hundred feet of the three stakes and wordlessly studied the ghoulish abomination. Though they were sickened by the sight of the bodies, they were helpless to drag their eyes away.

All three were naked, the stakes driven deep into

their bellies. The relentless heat, the collection of gases had ballooned them to twice their normal size. Decomposition already in progress, it was a feast of feasts for the flies, the hornets and other insects that swarmed nonstop about them. There was evidence—as they took in the other bodies scattered around the square—that desert foxes had found the picnic grounds as well.

Normally in these arid desert climes, properly cared for corpses could be wrapped in winding sheets, buried deep, the dryness of the air serving to preserve flesh and skin. Archaeologists constantly excavated such specimens, finding them parchmentized, their features still recognizable after twenty, thirty years in the ground.

But nobody had bothered to bury these pitiful villagers.

Manning killed the Land Rover engine. They all disembarked, commenced gingerly inspection of the village. As they came upon the first pitiful, fire-gutted hut, they recognized Blackwell's calling card. "Here we go," McCarter grunted angrily. "The son of a bitch wants full credit, don't he? Talk about flaming cheek...."

Inside each hut, down each meander of what passed for corridor between the blackened structures, they found charred, disintegrating deathly evidence of the madman's handiwork. The reek of death hung everywhere.

When they returned to the square, regarded the impaled figures one last time, Encizo said, "Christ, someone should cut them down."

"No, nobody touches them," Katzenelenbogen snapped. "The disease hazard here is high as it is." He sighed. "No, leave them. The buzzards should get whiff of them soon now." He glanced off to the highlands located some twenty miles to the west. "Why they aren't here by now, I don't know."

Keio Ohara, still green around the gills, turned away eagerly. "Let's get out of here, Yakov."

"I suppose. These poor people are beyond help."

The five men dressed in desert camos, wearing shorts, tan socks in their Raichle desert boots, matching camo slouch hats pulled down about their faces to ward off the worst of the sun, were in the process of returning to the Land Rover, when suddenly Encizo stopped dead.

"Freeze," he rasped, his eyes fixed on a huge sand dune flanking the eastern perimeter of the village. "I just saw something move. Someone's out there."

They broke pell-mell for the scout car, seized their assault rifles. Fanning out in precise, practiced maneuver, they advanced on the sector like flitting shadows. Had Blackwell been foolish enough to leave rearguard out there? There would be hell to pay.

Keio, his long, thin legs flashing, was the first to slog to the crest of the shifting sand pile. Flopping down just beneath the tip of the forty-foot-high dune, he flicked his head over the top. In the distance he saw two men desperately scrambling to crest another dune to the south.

"Relax," he called back to his comrades, "it's just a couple of natives we spooked. I'll go after them."

"Careful, Keio," Yakov called, frowning after the

impetuous Japanese, the youngest and least experienced member of the Phoenix team. "They might be armed."

There was a crisp rattle of gunfire, and Katzenelenbogen hotfooted it up the dune, arriving in time to see Ohara loping up behind the pair, turning them back with wide gestures of his M-16.

Five minutes later the first villager appeared, a dark brown man, perhaps sixty-five years of age, followed by a younger man in apparent distress.

"Look at that guy's hand," Encizo said. Nausea swarmed over him as he saw the swollen, blood-crusted, pus-dripping stump. "Or what used to be a hand."

"Quick," Yakov Katzenelenbogen snapped, "get that medical kit, McCarter." Yakov could appreciate the gravity of the maiming wound, since he, too, had lost a hand, his right, on a Middle Eastern battlefield. "We've got to help the poor devil."

He glanced at the terrified, bearded patriarch, concern in his gaze. "What happened to him?"

The thin, dry voice instantly replied in halting fractured English. "The men of Black Cobra. They chop his hand off. Blood Doctor. He cut it off when man refuse to join army."

Yakov's eyebrows rose. "You speak English?"

"Yes, I learn from my daughter. She went to mission school. If you are... patient I tell all."

The amputee hung back, recoiling in fear when McCarter returned with the medical kit. They tried to draw him closer. Feverish, eyes glazed, he was too weak for determined resistance. He began a pathetic pleading babble.

"Tell him we are trying to help him," Yakov said.

"He say do not want live. He shamed; he want to die."

"Die? But why?"

The old man explained the humiliating significance of a missing hand to a Muslim.

"What do we do?" Encizo asked Katz.

"We have to help him, if we can." He sighed and began to bathe the stump with alcohol.

He turned to Keio Ohara. "Fix me about a half grain of that morphine. I'm going to have to open that mess up again, cut the gangrene away. I've done corpsman duty in my time. Let's see if I can remember my basics."

Katz went on to explain the clean-away, the further paring of bone in order to gain enough healthy skin to form a flap over the stump, fasten it down with such crude stitches as the area would permit. "Even so," he added, "unless our friend has hospital care afterward he won't make it. And the nearest city that has one is El Fasher. Maybe someone can get him there. God knows, we can't."

The amputee went two shades whiter when he saw the syringe and realized it was meant for him. He made a feeble move to break free, but Encizo and McCarter caught him, held him fast.

"Tell him the morphine will deaden the pain," Katz told the older man, who could not believe that these white men were going to so much trouble on their behalf. "We must cut the rotten tissue away. Otherwise he will lose the whole arm, and he will more than likely die."

A long dialogue between the two Arabs followed, with the twenty-five-year-old protesting bitterly. But when the older man gave him what could only be interpreted as a tongue-lashing, the man became docile and agreed to the impromptu surgery.

The needle went into his arm. And while they waited for the morphine to cut in, they moved him toward the command car. There, in what shade they could manufacture, the man's stump braced on a 40mm cartridge magazine covered with a white T-shirt—maximum surgical sterility under the circumstances—the makeshift operation began.

Even in the shade the heat was intense, and Yakov was soon sweating bullets. The same with Rafael and McCarter, who held the patient steady, and Keio and Manning, who handed their Israeli ex-Mossad boss scissors, scalpel and nippers when he called for them, mopping his face at intervals. At close quarters the stench clouding up from the filthy wound was overpowering, and time and time again one or another of them gagged, verged on heaving.

The patient—though he could feel only barest twinges of pain—whimpered and cried out constantly until the old man held his hand over his eyes. Then the complaints ended.

The old man, who had by then introduced himself as Salibogo Mugunga, explained how he had found the maimed boy upon returning from a three-day fast and meditation session at a desert holy place. And with the discovery, knowledge came from the wounded man that his entire family had been wiped out. Wife, two sons, a daughter. . . .

Salibogo had tried to help the handless neighbor. He had washed and wrapped the stump, applied such folk remedies as were known to him. But nothing had helped, and the infection had only gotten worse. "Two days since Blood Doctor here."

Hearing the approaching Land Rover, thinking the Black Cobras were returning, he had fled into the dunes with his ward. Now, his voice grave, thick with emotion, he said, "*Allah yesallimek*—May Allah bless you—for I see you are a good man. You are decent men. We die you no come. We thank.... We thank...."

"You are most welcome," Yakov replied with matching respect, moved by Salibogo's fervor. "Is is the least we can do. After all that has happened to your village, to your people...."

The man's eyes glazed for a moment, then went clear again, a hard, vengeful determination growing behind them. He told them that one son, according to the wounded man, had been conscripted by the man they called Blood Doctor. The other son had been killed. His wife had been raped repeatedly; he had found her violated remains and had already buried her. But his daughter, Nemtala, he had not found.

"Blood Doctor," he finished, his voice ragged with misery, "he take her. Torture, rape, kill her, too, I know. I never see her alive."

"I am very sorry to hear that," Katzenelenbogen said lamely, not knowing how to respond to Salibogo's grief.

"Sorrow not enough," he replied gruffly, near-accusation in his tone. "Must give Salibogo a chance to become man again."

Katz paused in his slicing, bone-paring chores. "Yes? And how would I do that?"

"You let Salibogo come with you. I see guns. You fighting men, I know. You look for Blood Doctor?"

"Yes, we *are* looking for him," Katz replied.

"I help. I know countryside. I know language. I know customs of people. Teach me to shoot. I have gun. Hidden. I can kill Black Cobra soldiers. I avenge wife, sons. I avenge for evil he do Nemtala. Please? You take Salibogo?"

The rest of the Phoenix Force members were taken aback. Though deeply touched by the vehemence of the native's request, they recognized the complications involved. They all looked toward their headman where he worked so concentratedly—a one-armed man acting as savior to another one-armed man—waited on his reply.

"I don't know, Salibogo," Yakov said softly. "I don't know if it would work."

"We try?" the man pleaded, his eyes blazing with eagerness. "I make mistake, I fail you...you leave me. I ready die. If Salibogo fail, he die trying to avenge what evil Blood Doctor do to his family."

The pronouncement touched a sympathetic nerve. And how long, in this self-seeking world, had it been since they had heard someone offer to put his life on the line, risk all for those noble values closest to the human heart? Most people granted mere lip service to the tenets of freedom and justice. But how many lifted a finger to apply these lofty ideals? Again they hung on Katz's reply.

"Let me be, Salibogo," he snapped, his eyes angry. "I will think about it. That's all I can tell you now."

The old man fell silent, a grateful, small smile twisting his lips. He edged away.

Little by little the stubborn bones were chipped and snipped away. Millimeter by millimeter the necessary flaps of skin presented themselves. And now, thirty minutes later, Katzenelenbogen began to close up, using the suture thread from the medical kit. "He needs a transfusion in the worst way," he said, tying the final knot. "But how? We don't know his blood type. We don't have the equipment, anyway. I feel so helpless."

They made the amputee swallow some penicillin tablets; the stump was dusted heavily with sulfa powder, wrapped carefully in gauze. Very groggy now, barely able to stand, the man was helped into the back of the fast attack vehicle, arranged as comfortably as possible. Looking from the amputee to Katz, the men of Phoenix Force could not recall ever being more proud of their leader.

"Good job, Katz," McCarter said, forcing brusqueness into his tone. "Better than some hospitals I know."

"Hardly," Katz smiled, accepting the heartfelt compliment for what it was. "But we did our best. The poor man will go crazy with pain once the morphine wears off. We'll give him what we can spare, but when that runs out...."

Salibogo Mugunga, a small bundle of clothing and personal effects in his hand, an Arabian musket dating back a hundred years in the other, reappeared. "We go now?" he asked with a shy grin.

"Get in," Katz said grumpily, his pinched smile betraying his real mood.

3

For the next two hours, with Salibogo, the injured villager and Keio in the FAV, the rest in the Land Rover,
they proceeded slowly through the Libyan desert, trying to make the passage as easy as possible for their patient. Salibogo had informed them that the amputee
had family in Alliat, a Kababish village located about
fifty miles to the northeast; they hoped relatives there
would take him off their hands.

They paused for lunch in midafternoon, the awesome
heat at full fury. Sitting on the shady side of the vehicles,
they slapped the pumice-fine dust from their clothes,
scrubbed their faces with bandannas pulled from
around their necks. Again they forced the amputee to
drink as much water as he could take; it was crucial to
his condition. They tried to make him eat, but with the
pain building, he refused. Quickly they began breaking
out the Army C rations that they had found already
loaded in the LR when it had been dropped in Africa.

Salibogo talked of religious taboos when Keio shoved
his food packet in front of him. Yakov cut him short.
"You eat what we eat, understand? Otherwise we leave
you in Alliat with your friend."

Salibogo sulked briefly. "No eat. No go?" he repeated.

"You bet your sweet ass," McCarter intervened.

Salibogo ate. Sullenly at first, then with gusto as his hunger overcame his need to observe Muslim ritual.

And as they ate, as they downed water and salt pills, their strength and enthusiasm returned.

"Well, *señor*?" Encizo sent a mischievous sidelong glance to McCarter. "How do you like Africa so far? Do you find it as romantic and colorful as the travel brochures promised?"

"North Africa is the shits," McCarter grumbled, "and you damn well know it."

"Hotter than the hinges of hell," Rafael agreed.

There was silence then, the men chewing mechanically, staring into space, batting away the swarming sarcophaga flesh flies that constantly buzzed, persistently fought to land in their eyes, tried to crawl up their nostrils. The wail of the wind, the buzz of the insects, the muffled moans from the back of the FAV gave the impression that they had reached the end of the world. Perhaps they had.

Their mouths and noses felt as if they were stuffed with cotton, and they hawked up spit constantly. Their faces were scabbed, peeling, where the combination of wind and sand-reflected sunlight had already done its work despite all the sunscreen ointment they had plastered on their skin. Keio's ears were badly blistered because he had made light of wearing his hat until it was too late. Their noses were peeling, McCarter's especially. Katzenelenbogen, lightest-skinned of them all, had a forehead that resembled Death Valley in August.

Looking to the west, the towering dunes in prominent outline against the muted, shimmering profile of

Jebel Basira, they saw constant, blowing scrim of sand, the Sahara continuing its relentless southward advance on Chad and Sudan. To the east, in a waterless, snake-winding wadi they made out three withered acacias, the only sign of life the godforsaken landscape boasted. "And we've got eight hundred miles of this ahead of us?" Keio broke the silence.

The sound of a slap carried as McCarter fought the sarcophaga and sand gnats. "Bugger off, you bloody bastards," he growled.

Salibogo's head jerked up.

"Not you, mate," McCarter waved placatingly. "These bugs I'm talking about."

Salibogo nodded, a grin curving his lips.

"What about him?" McCarter whispered to Yakov. "Are we really taking him along?"

"Why not?" Yakov replied. "He's a good man. He means well. He might even save our lives one of these days. Lord knows my Arabic isn't all that sharp."

"Fine with me," McCarter, who had taken a quick shine to the tough old man, readily agreed.

"Same here," Rafael added. "He'll make a damned good scout. Loyal, that's for sure. He can ask questions we can't ask. We're gonna need all the help we can get in finding our tenderhearted friend, Blackwell."

The others continued to stare into the distance.

Hal Brognola had given a clear picture of just what kind of psycho Jeremiah Blackwell was during the Stony Man briefings four days ago. But he had not prepared them for the stomach-turning realities of the discovery at Abu Darash. His Marquis de Sade charisma, the blood-drinking—anything that might appeal to the superstitious African mentality they were apprised of. But the impalements, the destruction of an entire village. . . .

The grandiose adventure Blackwell had embarked upon also took some getting used to. To conquer all of Africa? To become the continent's new messiah?

"Hey—" Gary Manning, the normally taciturn Canadian, had interrupted Brognola's briefing "—you're putting us on. Conquer Africa? Blow up the Aswan Dam?"

But Brognola had not been kidding. Not at all. Even more eerie was that before he finished the comprehensive rundown, he had nearly convinced Phoenix Force that the Blood Doctor had a damned good chance of pulling the caper off. The Aswan Dam part of it anyway.

That was where Phoenix Force came in.

They had to find Blackwell's army, stop them short of the High Dam.

Brognola had provided a fix on Jeremiah Blackwell, age thirty-five, former paratrooper captain, 82nd Airborne Division, a product of Caxton, Alabama, who had been a renegade ever since his first exposure to "White Man's Justice." Each new injustice and slight had been stored away, left to fester in his subconscious, brewing into a murderous dementia, an implacable hatred for "Whitey."

When his father disappeared during the 1965 Selma, Alabama, freedom demonstrations and was later found in a stream bed just outside the city, his head literally shotgunned away, the seventeen-year-old learned a lesson that would remain with him until the day he died. The man with the gun is the man with the power. So he set out to get himself a gun. Many guns.

He did this by enlisting in the army at eighteen, turning himself into a model soldier—gung ho, by the book in every way. Somehow, he wormed his way into one of the army's most elite substructures—the paratroopers. There had been much made, at that time, of the lack of black officers in the military. So Blackwell exploited that angle and entered officers' training. By 1978, at age thirty, he had achieved a captaincy. His superior officers had all marveled at his total dedication, his intense preoccupation with weaponry, his complete immersion in the study of tactics.

He was a soldier's soldier.

When, in 1979, Flight Lieutenant Jerry Rawlings, of the Ghana Air Force, seized control of Ghana in a brilliant coup, Captain Jeremiah Blackwell found his role model; a new obsession was sparked in his psyche. But with important difference: where Rawlings fought an idealistic battle against wholesale corruption, Blackwell would battle for a power base alone. He would fight for ultimate power to force his warped will upon others, upon the whole world if possible.

By then, of course, he had gone around the bend.

Blackwell had resigned his commission in 1980. He had gone to Africa to begin establishment of his new kingdom on earth. He had received baptism of fire as a merc during the Angola–Zaire border conflicts. The experience served him well, honed his insights into

African psychology. Rawlings's persuasive skills paled into insignificance when compared to Blackwell's mesmerizing approach.

Blackwell knew how to rally the black man. His siren call was based on trading on terror for terror's sake—he promised opportunity to practice cruelty beyond all bounds of human decency. Revenge, endless bloodshed were all theirs if they enlisted in the Black Cobras, if they joined his infamous crusade.

Vindictive, exploited blacks bought it sight unseen. They flocked to his cause in droves.

There are ghouls who will sell their souls for that kind of carte blanche.

These ghouls soon formed the nucleus of Blackwell's officer cadre. And they, in turn, were shortly seduced by other truly professional ghouls, recruiters for Cuba's Dirección General de Inteligencia (DGI), infiltrating Africa in force to foment mischief for Russia's KGB. Blackwell and his officers had been dispatched to a terrorist-guerrilla university at Hauf, in South Yemen.

Even here Blackwell had managed to turn the tables on the *Cubanos*; he became exploiter, not exploitee. And where they intended to dispatch him on DGI missions in the Middle East, Blackwell had ideas of his own. One day he was in Yemen, the next he was back in Africa, deep inside Nigeria and Chad, regathering his forces.

Not only did he return with weapons, with the latest guerrilla techniques, he also returned with inside lines to the various African networks. He knew just which buttons to press to get the ear of the Rejection Front, the Polisarios, even top officials in Moammar Khaddafi's far-flung network. He would play one against the other, like pawns on Satan's chessboard. But he was not finished with the Cubans; they would also return to dance to his tune when he said so.

"The incredible thing—" Hal Brognola had finished that segment of their briefing "—is that Khaddafi, all those other guys bought it, lock, stock and barrel. They actually put up five million dollars for that bag of smoke. Not to mention weapons, ammo, vehicles for his campaign."

"Un-bloody-believable," McCarter gasped. "What in hell do Khaddafi and all the rest think they're going to gain by it?"

There was, Brognola went on, certainly no love lost between Khaddafi and Jaafar al-Nemery, president of Sudan. As they well knew. Nor between Khaddafi and Hosni Mubarak, Egypt's president. Both had gone against Libya with their continuing support of the Israeli peace offensive as signed by Anwar Sadat back in 1978. "We all know what the Rejection Front did to Sadat."

Nemery and Mubarak, though their nations were joined in a mutual defense pact, were very restless bedfellows. Each president had reasons for distrusting the other. Khaddafi had been increasingly itchy for invasion of Sudan of late; only the presence of U.S. AWACS in Egypt, the naval power standing off the Gulf of Sidra was holding him in check.

And so, to kill two birds with one stone....

Blackwell's troops would infiltrate Sudan, stage an attack across Egypt's border, smash the Aswan. The destruction of the dam would cause disaster to the

Egyptian economy, render the nation totally vulnerable to wholesale Rejection Front uprisings. Mubarak and his government would fall.

At the same time the desired Egypt–Sudan conflict would take place, and Khaddafi and company would come out of it with clean hands. The Egyptians, assuming that Blackwell had deliberately been given asylum in Sudan, or even that the treacherous al-Nemery had hired Blackwell himself, would declare war on Sudan.

"And just how does Blackwell propose to destroy the Aswan?" Manning had interjected. "That is one immense hunk of engineering. The biggest rock-fill dam in the world."

"We have to assume they will attack under cover of darkness," Brognola had responded. "Otherwise why the three hundred troopers? They'll seize the dam, rig high power explosives in crucial areas, and there she goes."

"Could they bomb it? Use a missile perhaps?" Manning asked.

"Highly unlikely," Brognola said. "They could, of course. But the question remains, why bother with the overland operation then? Why the miniarmy?"

"Tidy, very tidy," Colonel Yakov Katzenelenbogen mused. "Perhaps it's a bit too tidy. Why don't we just warn the Egyptian government that a raid is imminent, let them handle it themselves?"

"The term is tinderbox," Brognola had replied with a dour smile. "The CIA's intelligence has established that the roof's ready to blow off that part of Africa. All it will take is one small vibration."

"Which is?"

"Intelligence on either side that a secret force, read Jeremiah Blackwell, is in Sudan. Al-Nemery, in Sudan, will go off half-cocked against Khaddafi. Mubarak, in Egypt, will be at al-Nemery's throat. You can't begin to appreciate how precarious the situation is. One little explosion will set off a chain reaction that could easily trigger World War III. Undoubtedly America would be committed to maintain the status quo, and the moment that first Tomcat leaves the *Nimitz*, that's the moment the Soviets come in."

"So?"

"So it's a totally undercover operation. Once we drop you guys in Chad, you're absolutely on your own. End of communication. If you run out of supplies you live off the land. It's Phoenix Force and Phoenix Force alone. Only if Blackwell breaks out, closes in on the Aswan, will you be allowed to break radio silence, bounce a Mayday off one of our nearest satellites." His expression had become grave. "We are hoping that you get Blackwell first, that it doesn't get that close. How we'll salvage the operation if the dam does blow, I have no idea.

"This is your most dangerous assignment thus far. Mack Bolan is counting on you."

Six hours later Phoenix had lifted off from Stony Man's camouflaged airstrip, headed for Langley Air Force Base in Virginia. From there they had crossed the Atlantic in a Lockheed S-3A Viking, with a fueling stop at Lajes Field in the Azores. Thence on to Torrejon, a USAF–NATO base in Spain, where there had been a final briefing on the extra armor that Stony Man's armorer Andrzej Konzaki had designated for placement on their cross-country vehicles.

And finally, almost twenty hours after leaving Colonel John Phoenix's hideaway outside of Washington, D.C., they were airlifted by Sikorsky S-70 Black Hawk helicopter to a Chad drop site one hundred fifty miles northeast of Fada. Under cover of an ink-murky darkness, they had been dropped with pinpoint accuracy behind a monstrous sand dune. There, totally vulnerable and unprotected—delivered by a Boeing-Vertol CH-47 Chinook—the prestocked Land Rover and the FAV sat waiting for them.

A half hour later, Phoenix Force's private arsenal unloaded from the Black Hawk, and they were on the prowl. Cautiously they had closed in on the area where the Black Cobras had last been spotted by local counteragents.

A fruitless sweep had now brought them to this charming picnic grounds, where the men of Phoenix now finished lunch. Momentarily, as the last of their gear was packed, they paused to regard the FAV—a dune buggy actually, resembling a shallow bathtub on wheels—which they had dragged behind them for the past hundred ten miles.

With jaundiced smiles they considered the canvas-shrouded Mark 19 MOD-3 40mm machine gun mounted on the fast attack vehicle. Newly developed by the Marine Corps, it would soon receive its baptism of fire.

The 75.6-pound MG was capable of firing four hundred rounds of grenade cartridges per minute. With a sixteen-hundred-meter range, it could throw the most vicious flesh-shredders known to man. It had been chosen by Konzaki as the weapon to even out the sixty-to-one odds Phoenix faced against Blackwell's force.

The fast attack vehicle was another innovative weapon Konzaki had insisted upon. Designed by Emerson Corporation and just off the testing grounds, it had a flatland speed of seventy-five miles per hour. Powered by high-charge batteries, it could approach a firebase in spooky silence and take the enemy by total surprise—a decided tactical bonus. The electronics wizards at Stony Man had seen that installation of a series of polycrystalline-celled solar panels—plus special booster circuits—had been made. If the Libyan desert had anything, it had sun; thus the batteries would always be at peak charge.

Even so, Katz had insisted from the start that the lethal baby buggy be towed. The FAV must be at peak efficiency when the Phoenix cavalry answered that first bugle call.

Now Keio Ohara crammed his lanky frame into the FAV. Salibogo, dogging him like a shadow, a chipmunk grin on his leathery brown face, piled in beside him. "Let's haul ass," Keio called.

"Haul ass," Salibogo parroted.

McCarter goosed the Land Rover's starter, and the rugged, four-wheel-drive vehicle roared. Once more Phoenix Force was under way.

For the next hour they passed through desolate desert. No one spoke, the total emptiness of the terrain—nothing but ridged, wind-feathered sandhills stretching to the end of the world, seemingly—pushing each man deeper into private, doubting thoughts. Memory of the massacre encountered at Abu Darash still haunting, they chafed for action.

The afternoon wore down. Twice before they reached Alliat the Land Rover got bogged down where the hardpan of the narrow goat path was overrun by drifting sand. Much grunting, lifting, shoving, digging—and a profound wealth of cursing—got them out each time. But each setback taught new respect for the desert.

The handless man was at last delivered to his relatives in Alliat. Phoenix Force began hasty backtrack, hoping to find a main road—ageless caravan trail—that would provide hard evidence that Black Cobra forces had passed this way.

It was cooler now. The raw desert night was before them. They could expect temperatures in the midforties before the sun once again showed its mocking, hell-hot face.

The best they made in that stretch was thirty miles an hour. The wind gradually died, and the eerie stillness of the desert served to further unnerve them. At this rate Blackwell would blow the Aswan, meet them on his way back.

The sense of futility built, a kind of catch-up urgency and tension gnawing to the marrow of their bones.

Ahead of them the towering dunes stretched forever, a vast storm-tossed ocean of sand, wave cresting on wave with silent, frozen, taunting crashings.

And, God, they thought. Should they somehow suffer miscue, get lost in this everlasting wasteland. . . .

Phoenix Force doggedly pressed on.

4

Jeremiah Blackwell had the citizens of Al-Rashad stirred to a fever pitch. Four hundred strong, they crowded in the village square, cheered every word of the new prophet's diatribe. Blackwell stuck with his pidgin Arabic, keeping his speech simple. When a public execution was promised within the hour, a simple speech was all the madman needed.

He was talking a universal language.

He was talking hate.

Today's victim was a grossly fat, bearded Libyan merchant who had lived in Al-Rashad for only six years. Captain Angel DeRosa, the Cuban advisor assigned to Blackwell, had fingered the merchant for this particular propaganda effort. Dedicated advance man for the schizoid black's traveling circus, DeRosa had been in the village twenty-four hours prior to the main force's arrival. And he had uncovered a perfect fall guy.

What crime had Amal Jazirah committed against his fellow townspeople? Merely the crime of being the richest man. And some of his riches had been acquired illegally. Somewhere along the line, he must have cheated every villager at least once.

Jazirah was trussed like a Christmas pig, his hands

tied behind his back, ropes around his fat ankles. His turban askew, his clothes rumpled, he made a pathetic picture. Terror distorting his features, his eyes rolling pleadingly, his lips moved in whimpering entreaty every time there was pause in the black zealot's monologue. "I am innocent," he protested feebly. "I am an honest man. I have done you no wrong."

"You all know this man," Blackwell shouted. "You know that he has cheated you."

"Aywa, aywa," the villagers chanted. "Yes, yes."

"He has taken food from the mouths of your children," Blackwell prompted. "He has scorned and insulted your wives."

"He has stolen from us all," came the refrain led by shills deliberately placed in the crowd.

"He has taken improper liberties with your women?"

"Aywa," the crowd replied, surging forward in rage at the picture, totally false, that the black-uniformed officer so glibly painted. *"Aywa.* Let us have him. Let us kill him."

It was not as easy as all that. Poor Jazirah had a long way to go before punishment was meted out; Blackwell felt he must milk the moment of all possible emotion before he indulged their blood lust. He accused the sweating, cringing merchant of selling tainted food, of molesting children, of scorning the High Days. Blackwell said he was like all the rich, like all the white devils who backed him; he was heartless and cruel, he was an exploiter of the poor. He would not be happy until he had bled them all of every last piaster they owned.

"The white man," Blackwell raved, his voice rising to ragged pitch, "he is the cause of all our suffering. The white man must go. He must be toppled, killed, ground into the dirt."

"*Aywa*, the white devil must go," the crowd bellowed, the death fever mounting.

"That is why I have come." Blackwell smiled persuasively when the clamor subsided. "I have come to save you, to save Africa. Africa will once again become yours. Africa for the black man, not the white man.

"I am on a mission to the east," he went on, as if sharing a special secret with them. "But when it is finished, I will come back here. I will help you to fight the white man. Together we will defeat him. This country...your birthright...will be returned to you, the rightful owners."

So it went for the next half hour, Blackwell whipping the ignorant mob to a screaming frenzy. One moment his focus was on Africa's glowing future, the wealth each of them would acquire once the white man was vanquished. Next he vented his hatred on the cowering merchant, until the two issues became one, and the mob virtually swayed in a trance.

Somewhere along the line Blackwell craftily injected his main pitch, the recruitment of fresh troops for the Black Cobras. The pitch brought, as expected, a marked decrease in crowd fervor. Back to Jazirah's crimes. Back to a free Africa, an Africa in which they would all be rich, vested with many concubines.

Then, finally, the crowning stroke. "What would you have me do with this filthy bloodsucker?" he raged. "How shall he be punished?"

The usually docile and gentle citizens of Al-Rashad, caught up in the spell of a master of mob psychology, went amok. No punishment was too extreme now.

"Chop his head off. Cut off his hands. Disembowel him. Hang him." The suggestions came at rapid-fire pace. Blackwell knew he finally had them in his control.

Blackwell was nothing if not a man of his word. The hangman's rope appeared, the terrifying, long *panga* was produced and the thin pokers were plunged into the charcoal braziers that had been waiting from the outset. Bellows wielded by Black Cobra bullies turned the tips white-hot.

A table was lifted onto the platform where Jeremiah Blackwell and the sobbing, hyperventilating Libyan merchant were standing. His soldiers carried Jazirah to the impromptu torture rack. As he was untied, as he realized what they were going to do, the fat man screamed hideously and fouled himself before the chanting throng.

"For black Africa!" Blackwell bellowed, hyping the frenzied dementia. The machete came down with a vicious smash, and the man's left hand shot across the table, fell into the dust where it was retrieved by a babbling, wild-eyed citizen.

"For black Africa!" The fingers of Jazirah's right hand went hopping across the tabletop. Quickly the bully boys affixed tourniquets to each arm; the sacrificial cow must be made to last.

Before the dragged-out bloodfest was over, the man's eyes were put out and his tongue was pulled from his mouth with long-handled tongs. Finally, his throat was slit—Jazirah was long dead now—and the required bowl of blood was drawn. Blackwell ordered that what was left of the mutilated body should be hung by one foot in the top of the village's lone baobab tree.

Then came the grand gesture. "To black Africa," Blackwell intoned. The compound became deathly silent. Making great, slow show, raising the silver bowl of blood to the crowd, then to his lips, he drank the blood. When the bowl was empty, he smilingly faced the crowd.

Instantly his troops fell to one knee in the sand, forced all nearby natives to do likewise. "Blood Doctor," the low, spooky chant commenced. "Hail, all hail. Blood Doctor. . . ."

Blackwell waved the mesmerized mass to silence. "Where are the brave patriots of Al-Rashad?" he boomed, his voice a stirring battle cry. "Where are there twenty brave enough to fight at my side?"

At least fifty of the men in the square surged forward. Blackwell's lieutenants moved in and began singling out the more ablebodied, the youngest.

Shortly twenty-two males were cut from the jostling herd, escorted to their huts to gather personal belongings. They were then taken to a marshaling area and put under heavy guard; they would change their tune once the hysteria wore off. But by then it would be too late.

Later, as General Blackwell strolled through the village, congratulating the natives for the brave sacrifice they had made, he was joined by Captain DeRosa, the Cuban watchdog. "You were brilliant, General," he enthused, "absolutely brilliant. I have never seen you in such good form. You had them totally hypnotized. They were putty in your hands. Now if only the Aswan situation can be executed as brilliantly."

Blackwell glowered, a dangerous light clicking on behind his eyes. "You bastard," he snapped, his vehemence causing DeRosa to edge away from him. "I'll hold up my end of things; that pile of concrete is going down. If that fucking Castro kept his word half as well as I keep mine. . ."

"I meant no offense, General Blackwell. I. . . ."

"No big deal," Blackwell snorted, wandering off.

IT WAS 1940 HOURS and the desert dusk was at hand. Freshly bathed, shaved and wearing a clean uniform, Blackwell was coming down from the day's extreme high. Scarce as water was in the desert, he insisted on his daily bath and a fresh uniform. Tonight it was the royal blue, with gold fringe across the shoulders and chest. He wore a flamboyant peaked garrison cap—the Black Cobra insignia emblazoned in silver and black on one side—even though he sat indoors.

The cleanliness fetish, the love of gaudy uniforms—these were but a few of the Blood Doctor's quirks. Others would be revealed before the night was over.

Though he had already downed several stiff snorts of the Dewar's Scotch that was always kept stocked in his quartermaster trucks, he was still restive. Seeking some extra outlet to confer peace of mind, he let his thoughts drift to the lovely girl they had snatched at that last village. Blackwell was no womanizer; but tonight there was a need. He summoned Major Ochogilo.

"That babe you've got stashed away for me," he said. "Nobody's touched her, have they?"

"No, General," the fat clown reassured effusively. "Of course not. No one would dare. Your direct orders."

"Good. Get her cleaned up. Put some decent clothes on her. Deliver her here in exactly one hour."

The exotic, dusky-complexioned twenty-year-old beauty with the haughty eyes was named Nemtala—this much Blackwell had bothered to learn in the interim.

Her lustrous eyes were wide with fear as Ochogilo led her into Blackwell's quarters; her mouth was drawn to a thin, tense line. But still, even though she knew full well what to expect from him, she did not cower or cringe.

The gauzy, mint green, sarilike garment she wore emphasized her tawny coloring. And though the rustling gown concealed her lithe figure, it provided an aura of mystery, enhancing her desirability. Regarding her silently, gloating over the life-and-death power he held over the exquisite girl, Blackwell felt quick, itchy stirrings in his belly.

It would happen very fast. He was in no mood for games.

"I'm told that you speak English," he said finally.

"Yes, effendi," she replied in hushed tones, her eyes darting nervously. "I learned at a Christian mission school."

He sipped at his Scotch. He indicated the bottle.

"No," she said. "My religion forbids it."

"Never mind. I can do enough drinking for both of

us. Enough everything for both of us." His snicker
was ugly. "You know why you're here, don't you?"

She dropped her eyes. "I believe so, sir. To the vic-
tor belongs the spoils...."

He chuckled. "I think we're gonna get along just
great. I can use a smart woman to keep me company
once night comes on. Treat me right, and you'll make
out okay. Plenty okay. Enough of this shit. Over here,
Nemtala."

Nemtala swayed in place, her face registering a mixture of loathing, shame and terror. She made a brief
survey of the room, as if seeking an escape route.
Then, as suddenly, her expression went empty, stoic.
Moving like a robot, she started toward him.

Blackwell chuckled throatily and began blowing out
the candles in the room. Again seated in his chair, the
girl standing in stolid resignation before him, he began
to run his hands over her body.

Nemtala hissed, jerked. She fought to stifle the
tears, to swallow her cries of protest. There was
nothing she could do. He would kill her if she fought
him. It was the end for her.

Her tragic fate.

Blackwell grasped her by the hips, forcing her to
kneel before him. He began opening his trousers.

His hands closed on her shoulders, forcing her forward. When she whimpered, fought to pull away, his
fingers dug into her flesh like talons, sending a fireball
of pain shooting through her.

The helpless girl forced her mind to go blank. She
surrendered, let herself be forced to the vile act.

Her night in hell was begun.

SHE WAS UNCONSCIOUS by the time Blackwell was finished with her. Checking her pulse to see that she was still breathing, he smiled in the darkness. It was a forced smile. Deep inside, the man was suffering a rare torment of guilt.

He groaned and pulled further away from Nemtala. Yet fight the filthy pictures suddenly flashing on the screen of his brain as he might, he could not exorcise them. No, he raged. Please, not again.

Blackwell ducked his head, jammed the heels of his hands into his eyes, as if to physically obliterate the memories once and for all.

But they would not go away.

Once again he was a nine-year-old boy in Alabama, heading home from his backwoods school, with Marva, his eight-year-old sister in tow. Once more the three white-trash bullies, the boys all sixteen or older, were upon them, dragging them into the woods. Once more they were forcing him to undress, ripping away Marva's clothes as well.

They hit him again and again, twisted his arms, forced him to do sick things to his sister.

The remembrance of how they had made him rape Marva cut through his brain with jarring, cauterizing fury. He groaned, writhed in the tangle of his bedroll.

It had become his and Marva's secret. They had never mentioned that afternoon to each other again. The secret had gone to Marva's grave with her when she was killed in a school-bus crash in 1969.

As for Blackwell, he had managed to keep it stored in his subconscious. But sometimes the horror escaped.

With a muffled curse, he heaved himself up from the floor. "Ochogilo!" he roared as he pulled on his trousers and moved to light a candle. The man appeared, his smile turning sly as he appraised the crumpled, nude figure in the corner.

"Get that bitch outta here," Blackwell spat. "Outta my fucking sight. Have a party with her if you want. When you're finished, get rid of her. I don't ever wanna see her again."

"Thank you, General," he snuffled as he gathered Nemtala up and began edging from the hut, her body hanging limply in his arms. "A thousand thanks...."

The swarming bats were shrieking and fluttering inside Blackwell's brain again. He wanted to howl, to roll on the floor.

Instead he fell back onto the stool before the primitive table. He courted oblivion as he began knocking back shot after shot of Scotch.

5

Nemtala's eyes slowly opened. She shuddered, sucked in a quick breath. She realized she was no longer in the general's quarters; and the man forcing himself on her was not Blackwell.

Heart-searing despair slammed her. The total enormity of her degradation threatened to crush any last, lingering remnants of sanity. She did not want it to end with every man in the Black Cobra army using her.

No, she thought, recoiling. In the name of Allah, no! I won't let them do this to me. I will fight them. I will scream and claw and. . . .

But she did nothing of the kind. Instead she sank back in despair, allowing the fat, wheezing slug to continue his exertions over her. She struggled wildly to focus her thoughts, to arrive at some reasonable escape plan.

"So," Ochogilo snickered, never pausing for a moment, "the pretty little whore is awake? She finds that she enjoys being serviced by a real man? *Jayed, jayed.* It is good."

The man's breath, the reeking odor of his unwashed body almost did Nemtala in. Her stomach tipped; her head spun. Somehow she maintained control. But then, as she realized that Ochogilo had not even bothered to remove his clothes, she was further revolted. The pain, the hard object digging into her side, with each new thrust. . . . She slid her hand upward, to move the hard case or buckle away.

Her brain whirled as her fingers closed on what was the hilt of a short field knife, still nestled in its sheath. For a moment it seemed she could not breathe. As her fingers tightened on the weapon, the plan formed in her mind.

Ochogilo stirred as he felt her touch. "The haughty maiden begins to feel excitement?" he chuckled. "She finds that she needs a man after all? Yes, my pretty. Enjoy."

Nemtala sighed, feigning passion, letting her hands slide around his sweaty back, pressuring him to move faster.

The man muttered contentedly. He became so preoccupied with his pleasure that he never felt the sheath being opened, the knife being drawn from it.

Nemtala adjusted, sought greater leverage. One chance was all she had. And when the knife was poised to enter just beneath his right shoulder blade. . . .

It took all the strength she could muster to clasp her left hand behind Ochogilo's head, drag his lips down to hers. He groaned with pride as she crammed her mouth to his in sham ecstasy. Then the knife slammed down. Simultaneously her lips closed on his with sucking greed, her teeth clamped, clung to his lips for dear life in attempt to stifle his scream.

The knife rose and fell, rose and fell. Her teeth tore and lashed, the taste of his blood in her mouth sweet beyond description.

Ochogilo was released, allowed to flop off her body with a bubbling, sighing grunt. She wanted to shrill her joy as she heard the air hiss from that human balloon.

For a long time she sat over the man, regaining her breath, the smell of his puddling blood—a coppery, metallic odor—seemingly everywhere.

It was at that moment she heard a discreet rapping on the door. "Major Ochogilo?" the male voice called softly. "Almost through? We are waiting. Let us know when you have had your fill."

"One moment," she called in Arabic. "We will be finished shortly."

"As you say, miss."

Instantly she was up, her eye plastered to the hut's loosely hung door. She was chilled to the heart by this near-fatal mistake. She had never dreamed there would be more of the scum so close. In the half darkness she saw two men huddled in patient vigil just outside the door.

Moving decisively, realizing that delay could spell disaster, she managed to roll Ochogilo's body to one side, covering it with a blanket. She went to the door and stood behind it. "Major Ochogilo asks that one man come in now," she said in quavery, yet enticing voice.

The soldier came into the dark room, closed the door behind him quickly, paused to let his eyes become accustomed to the gloom. "Over here," she slurred softly.

The man was too busy opening his clothes to notice her evasive action. He advanced with a rush. When her fingers fluttered seductively upon his lips, he was further taken in. But then, the hand closed over his mouth, the knife slashed upward in swift, corkscrewing stroke, taking him full in the belly.

He tried to moan, but the hand tightened, and the knife plunged again, higher now, penetrating his heart. With a glug-glugging sound—combined croak of dismay and death rattle—he slumped to the floor.

Shortly he, too, was snuggled up next to his mate beneath the blanket.

Nemtala let an appropriate period of time pass, hoping that her faked murmurings of sexual delight would lull the remaining soldier. Finally she moved to summon the last man.

She chanced an outcry this time. The man was hardly inside the room, the door closed behind him, when she flung herself from the shadows like an avenging angel.

He went down with a ragged grunt, flopped, rolled. His mouth opened wide, a hoarse shout beginning to build. But the knife sang a hissing death song.

Five minutes later, all the bodies concealed beneath blankets and bedrolls, Nemtala was ready.

When she finally slid out into the night she wore a black, baggy uniform, boots, a Black Cobra cap. She began moving through the dense darkness. When a staggering soldier appeared, she ducked back. As he passed she scuttled forward again.

She cursed the weight of the two AK-47s she carried, the added burden of two cartridge belts. But they were essential. If she was ever to avenge herself on the Black Cobra general who had defiled her. And avenge herself she would. She swore it by all that was sacred to her.

Not now, perhaps. But, somehow, one day.

She darted from hut to hut, working her way toward the outskirts of Al-Rashad. Dogs barked, sniffed her heels, but the soldiers, the animals' owners, paid them no heed. From a distance the rumble of male voices—laughing and singing—carried. The *pomba*—native beer—was doing its potent work. Nobody would be alert for runaways this night.

She came to the last hut, took swift fix on the diamond-glittering stars. She was cold, deathly weary. Suddenly she was terrified of the trek that lay before her. But she shrugged away despair and doubt, somehow put tiredness aside. Doggedly she forced herself out into the desert, moving as fast as her wobbly legs could carry her.

Nemtala knew she had to be many miles away from the camp by dawn when the slashed bodies of the terrorist trio would be discovered.

She found a road and picked up her pace, hewing to the hardpan so her tracks would be difficult to find.

A frenzied determination on her face, she headed due west, toward what was left of Abu Darash.

6

Salibogo was the first to hear the noise. His hearing was amazing for a man of sixty-five. He abruptly lurched up beside Keio Ohara in the FAV, strained his neck, almost as if sniffing the air.

"Hey, old man," Keio said, instantly alerted. "What's up?"

"Guns. I hear shot. Far off."

It was 1030 hours, and Phoenix had been slogging its way deeper into Sudan since 0600 hours. Already the heat was climbing to new, insufferable highs. Keio flung himself from the dune cart and raced up beside the lumbering Land Rover.

"Kill the engine," he yelled at McCarter, who was playing chauffeur this morning. "Someone's shooting out there."

McCarter flipped the key, touched the brakes. Instant silence.

Each man at battle alert, swiftly transformed into a superb fighting machine, Phoenix became coiled steel. Eyes darted.

The rattle of rapid fire carried clearly in the sterile, arid atmosphere. It died momentarily, then took up. Again it died, leaving them with only the sound of their harsh breathing and the moaning of the wind.

"Damn," Encizo said, "don't tell me we got lucky. Have we found the bastards already? How many do you think, Yakov?"

"Hard to tell. Could be a rearguard group. Could be the main force. There's only one way to find out.

"Keio," Katz snapped. "Unhitch the FAV. We finally get to see what that albatross can do. Well, gentlemen. Whenever you're ready."

The men of Phoenix Force did not have to be told twice. They scattered, slapped on cartridge belts, personal leather and unlimbered SMGs from every available nook and cranny in the Land Rover.

There was even an extra M-16 for Salibogo, who, under McCarter's tutelage the past two days, had become an excellent marksman. The old man's eyes sparkled, his face wrinkling into a grin as the rifle was thrust at him.

The FAV key was turned over. The fast attack vehicle lurched forward, accelerated to forty in as many seconds, a phantom wraith streaking along the rutted, steeply canted camel trail.

They were doing sixty before they had covered a mile.

"Hang on, you goldbricks," Keio hooted, ripping the wheel back and forth viciously to avoid the worst potholes. "The Marines have landed."

Shortly the headlong pace was tamed. A fresh tattoo of rifle fire echoed among the dunes, then died out. The racket was closer, and a feverish, gut-tightening tension infected the attack force.

"Hold her down, Keio," Yakov snapped. "No telling what's around that next bend." As they approached a last sandpile defilade, Katz instructed Keio to pull over. "Recon, guys. On the double," Katz said to Manning and Encizo.

The two flung themselves out of the FAV, slogged down the right side of the trail. As they neared a fifty-foot-high dune that flanked the ragged-ass excuse for a road, they made last-minute adjustments to their rifles—Encizo on the Stoner M-63 A1, Manning packing a Heckler & Koch G3 this mission. Satisfied with their at-ready status, they began climbing the dune.

The rest of the team watched intently as they climbed.

Encizo and Manning paused beneath the lip of the dune. With slow, careful scoopings they began forming a notch in the ridge before them. For long, frozen moments they stared out at the trackless wastes below them. Satisfied, they began sliding back down, setting off sand avalanches on their way.

"They're back in the dunes about a half mile away," Rafael reported. "I saw about ten of them, but there has to be more back in there somewhere. What they're shooting at, I don't know. I didn't see anything."

"Blackwell's boys?" Yakov snapped.

"Seems so. Tan camos, black caps. All holding AK-47s."

"Two Unimogs alongside the road about a thousand yards ahead," Manning interjected. "Stupid apes left them totally unprotected." He grinned. "Spoils of war."

"So it's not the main force apparently," Katzenelenbogen said. "We can take them."

"We've still got road cover for another half mile,"

Manning continued. "There's a hard ridge that follows the dune line we can use if we like. We'll be up their asses before they even know we're on the scene."

"Sounds good," Katz said. "Keio. Move this baby buggy."

As they eased out, the gunfire built up again. Now everything fell silent. "They've got somebody pinned down back there," Encizo said. "I pity the poor bastards. *Who*, I wonder."

"We'll soon find out," Keio muttered, slowly edging the FAV another two thousand feet down the narrow ruts.

"Manning," Katz said as they reached maximum penetration into enemy territory and made a move to veer into dune country, "take charge of the Unimogs. Blast them with their own MGs if they come your way. Don't let any of them escape."

Manning nodded, then cautiously began working his way toward the deserted assault vehicles.

Phoenix Force started the slow climb into the dunes. Salibogo proved invaluable. With lifelong knowledge of the terrain, he was able to point safe passage through the sand and keep the FAV from being bogged down.

At the base of another towering dune, the FAV hummed to sudden halt; Phoenix Force began hasty deployment.

Katz ordered McCarter and Keio to disengage the Mark 19's pintle from the pedestal mount and to haul the seventy-six-pound piece, along with two fifty-pound magazines, up a lower dune to the west. Mounting the MG on an independent tripod, McCarter was assigned to waiting detail.

"We'll be flanking them," Katz explained, "driving them in your direction. So don't go falling asleep, my friend."

"That'll be the flaming day," he retorted.

Next, following a terse strategy briefing, Katz led Encizo, Ohara and Salibogo to the south. Each man maintaining a hundred-foot interval, they began a wide sweep of the cluster of dunes. Keying on the sporadic gunshots, the long scarrings in the sand, which Blackwell's troops had left behind, they converged on the main force. Finally—the four-man team dispersed to murderous advantage—Katz waved them forward. Legs pumping, sand sliding, fighting for balance, they began clawing their way up the steep incline.

Upon nearing the top they stopped and again carved a peephole into the edge, silently observing the bewildering scene below.

There were approximately twenty Black Cobras sprinkled across the sun-glared desert. Even as Phoenix Force watched they saw the Cobras shooting at random—into the ground, against the opposite walls of the concave arena.

Katz's dismay grew. What were the silly asses shooting at? Snakes? Sand ants?

The black troops paused in their efforts and began working their way up the next hill. Katz, hoping perhaps to acquire interrogation material, chose to challenge them. *"Wakkif,"* he roared in Arabic. "Halt! Drop your arms or die."

There was no way the hardened mercs were going to surrender without a fight. Instantly the desert was a fire garden, the men whirling, falling sideways, the Kalashnikovs baying sharp, metallic chants, 7.62mm deathmakers whining through the air above Yakov's head, hammering the sand embankment before him, jetting clouds of sand into his face.

On each side of Katz, the remaining Phoenix warriors opened up, pouring a deadly, withering rain of hot lead into the enemy, almost immediately reducing the number of the Black Cobra squad by half.

One terrorist, hammering his boots into the sand, almost made it to the top of the dune. But a 5.56mm bullet from Encizo's Stoner homed in on the back of his skull. He flung up his arms, threw his AK-47 over his head, then slid down the incline.

Another hardguy, zeroing in on Yakov, took a hot kiss from the Israeli's left, as Salibogo stitched him across the throat with three deadly accurate rounds. He lurched upright, executed a quick pirouette, then pounded his face into the ground.

A Black Cobra hardman flopped, rolled and hysterically stuffed great handfuls of sand into his gut where Keio's M-16 had nearly disemboweled him.

Another of Blackwell's elite bullies ran in quick, manic circles, his eyes gone. Another burst from Yakov's Uzi, and he was suddenly beyond pain.

Another six bodies lay motionless in the large sandbox. All had checked out during the first lead raindown.

Yakov signaled his men to hold their fire and again offered amnesty to the hard-core cases. "Throw down your guns," he roared. "You still have a chance to live."

Apparently surrender was a dirty word to the remaining Black Cobras, and they still kept clawing the walls of sand, hoping against hope that somewhere there was a hiding place for them. Salibogo and Keio, firing in tandem, spurred them into a spastic African death dance.

Those who made it to the top of the dune to the far west also might as well have saved themselves all that work. They had no sooner scrambled over the top of the hill than they were immediately propelled backward as McCarter opened up with the Mark 19. The cartridge grenades chopped holes in their backs big enough to accommodate a man's fist.

"Watch it, Katz," Encizo bellowed as a pair of Black Cobras abruptly popped up on the battlescape's northern periphery. The terrorists blasted on full automatic and pulverized the comfy pocket where he had just been. Even as the stunned Israeli rolled down the incline, fighting for purchase every foot of the way, the hardmen tried for killing shots, oblivious to the others zeroing in on them.

Three SMGs opened up at once. The terrorists executed a sideways shuffle before going down, literally torn in half at the middle.

There were still survivors. Three Black Cobras miraculously fought their way from the desert Dunkirk and somehow managed to topple over the crest of the dunes to the south. Katz fought to his feet and tried to stop them, but his shots went wide. "Down, Yakov," Keio called. "I've got a shot here."

For the second time Yakov ate dirt as the M-16 tumblers sliced the air three feet above his head. The hardmen managed to put another dune between them and Phoenix's main contingent.

They were home free. Or so they thought. Emerging from behind dunes a thousand feet away, they broke for the waiting Unimogs. Keio could hear their jabber as they raced toward the transport vehicles—and deliverance. Once they got behind their own heavy guns. . . .

Manning moved up from his hiding place behind the cab, swung the Russian Goryonov MMG down on the sprinting terrorists. They saw him too late. They swung up their Kalashnikovs and tried to get shots off. The muzzle-flash was blinding, even from a distance, and as the supervelocity 7.62mm rounds connected, the Cobras were stopped in their tracks, blown backward a full five feet, parts of them sent flying over the desert.

A long, stunning silence hit the desert, and up in the dunes the men of Phoenix Force sank to the ground in momentary collapse. Sweat streamed in buckets, drenching them; they fought for breath, their intake hoarse, sucking. The damnable heat. They stared around them, regarded the newly created human garbage with haunted eyes.

But finally the spell was broken. And hearing McCarter's voice, they stirred up. "Is everything all right up there? Do you guys give up?"

"Yeah," Encizo called. "We give up. Spare our women."

Still none of them moved. It had all happened so swiftly. Just what had those guncocks been doing there?

A jarring rifle crack jolted them back to reality, and

all swiveled, rifles poised. They saw Salibogo walking from terrorist to terrorist, sending a final round into each man's brain. A curse in Arabic, a gob of spit in each face. On to the next man.

"Damn you, Salibogo," Rafael roared. "Knock that off. Stop it, do you hear?"

The wizened Arab stared back at Rafael, sincere dismay in his eyes. Reading the fury in his friend's eyes, he shrugged and quit his cruel sport.

But Salibogo was nothing if he was not practical. His eyes glistening with savage satisfaction, he trudged from fallen soldier to fallen soldier, retrieving AK-47s, cartridge belts, until he nearly staggered under the load. Modern weapons were worth their weight in gold in the desert. They meant the difference between slavery and freedom.

Katz, Keio and Encizo shook their heads patronizingly. Let the old man do his thing.

They started from the pit of death. "Hold your fire, McCarter," Encizo bellowed as they climbed up the western side of the swale. "We're coming over."

There was a slight plateau at the top of the dune, a miniature depression.

They turned back to watch Salibogo divest himself of the weapons, immediately facing east, prostrating himself on the sand. Rafael rolled his eyes. Prayers?

Salibogo commenced a muffled, chanting prayer.

They were totally unprepared for what happened next. In a ruffled, uneven spot in the sand, the ground actually opened up, and a figure—covered with sand, sweeping away a head-wrapping, spitting and blinking—sat up before their eyes.

Their assault rifles came up, but they managed to hold their fire. Eyes bulged. Jaws fell in silent gape.

As the slightly built Black Cobra flung himself toward Salibogo, fell upon him, wrapped his arms lovingly about the old man's back.

"Tshar-raf, ya abui," the apparition in black wailed, the voice definitely female. A wailing, sobbing, totally distraught female. "Most honored father. I have found you. Your dishonored daughter has returned at last...."

Salibogo straightened from his prayers, stared at the dirty, bedraggled creature, searched the desperate eyes. "A miracle," he gasped, his voice cracking with emotion. *"Mahboob, ya bint...ya tifil...* Nemtala, my beloved daughter, my child...returned to me. Allah is good."

While the two figures clung in embrace, rocked and sobbed, the members of Phoenix Force stared at each other in utter astonishment. Just what in hell was going on, their baffled eyes demanded.

7

The trick, as Salibogo eventually explained it, was as old as the Koran; nomad children were taught it from early on. When there was danger from an opposing tribe, when the slavers came, the children were instructed to run into the desert and bury themselves in the sand.

This was explicitly explained by every parent; each child had to perform a dry run under his father's watchful eyes. A deep hole was scooped into the desert, the sand carefully piled to one side. All clothing was pulled tight, the face wrapping was wound, leaving only a tiny hole at the mouth. The individual then arranged himself in the depression, began covering his body from the feet up, smoothing the sand over himself as he went. Finally the head and upper shoulders were buried, the hands being left for the very last.

Sand was smoothed at every step; any obvious buildup was a dead giveaway. When the ground was as level and smooth as possible, the arms were finally drawn in. A well-practiced vibration procedure followed, the buried person shaking for prolonged periods, causing further sift-down, making the hiding place indistinguishable from the rest of the desert.

To breathe, the person used foot-long reeds, which were collected at oases. The reeds were placed between the lips, poked out inches above the level of the sand. A person could survive for hours, until danger had passed.

"So that's what those bastards were doing—" Encizo smiled in numb appreciation of Nemtala's stunt "—when they were shooting up the dunes. I thought the sun had finally got them."

Nemtala had used the gimmick twice during her flight from Al-Rashad, Salibogo explained. Each time she had managed to evade the party Blackwell had dispatched after finding Ochogilo and his stooges dead. But each time they had somehow managed to pick up her trail and had dogged her relentlessly.

Only upon hearing the familiar Muslim prayers and recognizing her father's voice had she thought it safe to rise from her sandy grave.

McCarter's tone was admiring. "That's what I call a tough girl," he said. "After the hell she went through. Then to kill them buggers, steal their fucking weapons to boot. To make her way back here. I'm sure as hell glad she's on our side."

Nemtala had withdrawn into a sullen, watchful silence once the reunion with Salibogo and the brief rundown on details of her escape from Blackwell two days before were finished. Her eyes haunted, she needed a long sleep in the worst way.

Whenever one of the Phoenix team got close she shuddered, appeared to shrink inside her grubby clothes. She cringed, avoided their eyes, despite her father's repeated assurances that these were good men, kind men. The very men responsible for saving his life—*her* life, for that matter.

After answering Katz's questions about Jeremiah Blackwell's location, his route and possible destination, Nemtala shyly requested some water to clean herself.

There was water, she was told. Especially after capture of the Black Cobra vehicles. Water to waste. Soap, towels, even extra, fresh clothing were provided, the latter from Katz's duffel—he was the smallest Phoenix member. Manning returned to the dunes and came back with a pair of boots small enough to fit her.

While Nemtala bathed behind an improvised tarp, the rest of them transferred water and fuel supplies from one Unimog to the other. Salibogo, of course, would not be content until every rifle and round of ammo was gathered and flung into the Unimog they would take along.

The abandoned Unimog was expertly gutted, set on fire. The Black Cobras—twenty-two in all—were left where they had fallen, consigned to the mercies of the blazing sun—and the buzzards.

An hour later, they were loading up. Manning would drive the Unimog, with Salibogo proudly ensconced beside him. A place had been cleared in back where Nemtala could sleep.

As she appeared, dressed in Yakov's tan camo top, shorts and socks, the boots on the large side, she struck a surprisingly fetching picture. Her long black hair wet and glistening, her curves visible even through the baggy military issue, she sent a timid smile as she appeared. Quickly she scurried to climb up behind

Salibogo and disappeared into the back of the Unimog.

"Hey, now," David McCarter chuckled, "that's a bit of the all right, ain't it, mates? Adds a touch of class to the joint, wouldn't you say?"

Manning nodded, then gunned the Unimog engine.

Once more Phoenix Force set out.

In the Land Rover, seated beside the driver, Katzenelenbogen was busy with his charts. He hummed tunelessly to himself, an unmistakable signal that he was distressed. "What's it look like, Yakov?" Encizo asked, leaning over the back of the seat, studying the quadrant maps with him. "We any closer to catching up with that slimeball?"

"Hardly," Katz said, his lips pursed. "He's still got four days on us. If I can go by what Nemtala told me, he was here, at Al-Rashad, two days ago." He indicated a point on the map. He flipped the drafting compass, took in an equal distance to the west of the hamlet. "Which should put him here, somewhere near Abu Tabari."

"Did Nemtala give you any clue where he's heading?" McCarter joined in.

"She was a bit vague, sad to say. But she did hear some mention of Jebel Oda. Which is here, practically on the Red Sea, about two hundred miles south of the Aswan Dam. At elevation two thousand, it provides some of the worst fighting terrain you could ask for. And if you think this desert is tough, wait until we hit the Nubian desert. Rock there that will chew our tires to shreds. Wadis we'll never get out of."

"Sounds bloody charming." McCarter laughed. "We've all had things too damned soft of late."

"Otherwise Nemtala says that Blackwell's well organized," Katz went on, "that his men are fanatics, well-disciplined robots who'll follow him to hell and back. Oh, yes. They travel mostly by night, sleep by day. Their camouflage people are, apparently, experts. Once they set up a base nobody spots them again."

He grunted. "So, even if we had Grimaldi or somebody up there, doing air recon, it's more than likely that we'd never find trace of them."

"So?" Encizo prodded. "What do we do?"

"Play it by ear. With this damnable dead-air policy Brognola has imposed, we're virtually reduced to Stone Age tactics. Follow our nose and hope for the best. If worse comes to worst, we can always key on Jebel Oda and pray that we get there at the same time Blackwell does."

"Mighty slim odds," McCarter said.

"Have you got any better ideas?" Katz frowned.

"Can't say that I have."

So the long day passed, Phoenix somewhat heartened by knowledge that they were basically on track, that, if there was such a thing as a just God, they would catch up with the Black Cobras in due course and settle some nasty scores.

At midafternoon they came upon a band of nomads. They stopped briefly while Salibogo questioned them. Studying the primitive family unit, seeing the malnourished children—impassively staring, oblivious to the swarms of flesh flies that formed dark rings around their eyes and mouth—they wondered what pleasures, if any, life held for the nomads.

What could the average life expectancy be in these

godforsaken backlands? If the tsetse flies and their various forms of encephalitis did not get you, then the water would. The bilharzia parasite was everywhere, infecting eighty percent of the population.

From the outset Phoenix had been warned about the drinking water. Even Salibogo (among the more enlightened of his brothers) harped constantly on this. They boiled the water for a half hour; for good measure they faithfully added the Halizone tablets that Stony Man had provided in their survival kit.

Abruptly Salibogo interrupted the wordless staredown between the commando team and the sadsack nomads. "They know nothing," he reported to Katzenelenbogen. "They have seen no strangers except for us. They have been in desert for many weeks. Let us go on."

The Land Rover roared, lurched forward. Gradually they shifted into third gear, reached a speed of thirty-five, the vehicle rolling viciously as they fought to stay on the road's high ridges. The stiff springs transmitted every rut, jolted them nonstop, seemingly loosening teeth, disconnecting hip joints. Here the wind had eroded deeply, left a washboard of stone, the gaps two feet wide.

Low gear. Five miles per hour.

"God almighty," McCarter complained. "I feel like the cork ball in a bobby's whistle."

The wind picked up toward 1700 hours, and the trail became obscured by blowing sand. Still they pressed on, eating dust, spitting, wiping the tiny particles from blood-streaked eyes. They could only hope that Blackwell was encountering similar conditions.

They stopped in a village called Gahwak—a sorry collection of eight stick huts, a thorn-tree palisade to contain a herd of six cows—which boasted a population of twenty-six starving souls. Again there was no report of passing strangers. If the Black Cobras had come this way they had deliberately bypassed the village.

Blackwell, the wily bastard, was not about to advertise his unauthorized presence in Sudan.

They made another thirty miles before daylight began to fade. There was pause for chow. Again there was dust-off, prolonged spit-fest. But no scrub down. Katz decreed that they would put in another six hours before sack time. They could crash for a few hours sometime after midnight.

There was no grumbling. If eighteen-hour-days allowed them to gain on Blackwell—go for it. They had come to Africa with a mission in mind.

They sat in close huddle, saying little, chewing the tasteless rations, gulping harsh, black coffee, which Salibogo prepared. Steaming hot in Arab tradition, the coffee almost seared away the roofs of their mouths. Yet it was satisfying, especially with the first chill of the desert night coming on.

Sipping the scalding brew, they noticed that Manning had disappeared. A walk in the desert, they mused. But they were mistaken, for shortly he returned, a stiff smile on his face, his mess tin in his hands.

"I tried to get Nemtala to eat," he said, his tone carrying concern. "But she didn't want anything. Poor kid, she's bushed. Scared to death of me."

THE FIRST LIGHT OF DAWN had barely made itself known to the horizon when Katz stirred from his sleeping bag, shrugged into his clothes and began making the rounds. He nudged each man where he slept on the ground.

Behind the Land Rover Salibogo was already clattering the primus stove. The temperature stood at forty-five degrees.

Grumbling, the men crawled from their bedrolls, began their morning washup, such as it was. There was not a hell of a lot they could do on a quart of water apiece, but amazingly they made it stretch. Shivering in the muted light, they stood and scrubbed vigorously. Shaving, of course, was out of the question. Or was it?

"Will you look at that?" Encizo dug Ohara in the ribs. They both stared over at Manning, who had heated his water ration and was sawing at his stubble with a razor.

"Someone's got ideas," Keio smirked.

They were on the trail an hour later, the Land Rover in the lead, the FAV in tow, the Unimog grumbling in the rear, all spaced apart to minimize dust blowback. The men yawned, drew field jackets tighter, fought to clear sleep-muddled heads. Gradually the day's heat built.

Another mangy village rose like a mirage from the desert at 1040 hours. The answer was the same: no one had passed.

At the village, Nemtala finally awoke, came forward to the Unimog and held a whispered conference with Salibogo. She studiously put distance between herself and Manning, sitting on the seat's outer edge. She ravenously tore chunks from the oversized doughnut-shaped loaf of bread—*ka'ak*—that her father had purchased from one of the village wives.

Once more they set out.

They stopped for lunch at 1230 hours. Nemtala, less standoffish, her color definitely better, an inner glow of vitality returning, took the food that Manning offered and ate.

Nevertheless she hung close to her father and regarded the hard-eyed crew apprehensively. When McCarter and Ohara attempted to joke with her, she sent quiet, imperious glances their way, but made no reply.

"Talk about frostbite. . ." Keio remarked.

There was curious change of status as Phoenix moved out this time. Nemtala, though still owlish and silent, now chose to sit between Salibogo and Manning.

They reached Al-Rashad, birthplace of Nemtala's infamy, at 1500 hours, and she became more edgy with each approaching mile. "It's all right," Manning repeated in slow careful phrasing. "Nobody will hurt you. We'll be beside you to protect you. It's all right."

Salibogo went in first—the convoy standing off a mile away, concealed by a sandy bluff—to get the lay of the land. A half hour later, as he reappeared, waved them ahead, the engines were revved up.

Once Phoenix was inside the small town—the villagers were definitely uneasy over the presence of a second military convoy in a few days—there was a concerted recon by Salibogo, with Katzenelenbogen in tow to provide the necessary muscle.

Seeing the mutilated, rotting body still hanging in the branches of the baobab tree, McCarter made a sour face. "This must be the place. Looks like our jolly butcher friend's been here."

Again there was a quiet conversation between Nemtala and her father. Moments later, the AK-47 hanging menacingly on his shoulder, he followed her into the village's woebegone souk. Salibogo drove a hard bargain as his daughter picked out items of clothings. She looked pleased as she climbed aboard the Unimog, secreted her purchases in one corner of the truck box.

"Blackwell pulled out three days ago," Katz informed the others as they clustered at Al-Rashad's primitive well and topped off their water tanks. "Took a gang of their young men along with them. The townspeople are definitely angry. Blackwell had approximately three hundred men." He paused. "Minus twenty-odd as of yesterday. I expect he'll pick those up along the way. Has quite a persuasive way about him, I hear."

All eyes drifted to the baobab tree.

His smile became confident. "So. Three days. We're making progress of sorts."

An hour after reaching Al-Rashad, they were on their way again. The sun bore down with blistering fury, and even in the shaded LR, the men sweated like steelworkers, their uniforms plastered to their bodies, rimed with salt. The sweat provided a base for the dust, and they were again coated.

Back in the Unimog, Nemtala, breathing easier once Al-Rashad was behind them, loosened even more. Her black hair coiled in a lush bun, a heavy burnoose-type covering draped around her head, she had a dusky, exotic appeal, which Manning found quite unsettling.

Manning was surprised when—a half hour under way—she addressed him. Her English was lilting, charming. "You have name, effendi?"

"Manning," he blurted, his pulse racing for no good reason. "Gary Manning. Call me Gary."

"I am called Nemtala. Those who are friends call me Tala. You would call me Tala?"

"Yes...Tala."

"You have been very kind...Gary. I want you to know your concern has been appreciated. I have been...I am so afraid."

"You have good cause. Not many girls...women would have the courage to kill...to come out of that situation the way you did. I...we all admire your bravery."

There was a long silence. But her faint smile betrayed her pleasure at his praise. "You bring me food," Tala said softly. "You build shade place for me sleep. You are good man, I think."

"Thank you, Tala. It was the least I could do."

"Please, effendi...Gary. You do one more thing for me? A favor, I think you call it?"

"Certainly. What is it?"

Her eyes dropped. When she looked up again, they were clouded with a hard, unreasoning glitter. "That man in Al-Rashad. He do evil things to me...he force me to do evil things. I am unclean. I have been shamed beyond recall."

"Don't, Tala," Manning protested gently, his heart filling with sudden compassion for the tormented woman. "Try not to think about those things. You are not shamed. You couldn't help what happened to you."

Her stare was implacable. Her voice was eerie, muffled, a paranoid note creeping into it. "I do not care what you say. I am dishonored. I will be avenged. I want to kill that man, fix so he will never hurt another woman again."

The steely vehemence in her voice caused Manning to shiver. He was momentarily at a loss for words.

"There are many guns back there." She tossed her head backward. "Much ammunition." Her eyes flared, locked in his. "The favor, Gary. . . ."

"Yes?"

"You teach me to shoot. You give me chance to kill that animal?"

8

Nemtala proved to be an excellent pupil. Morning, evening—virtually every time they stopped—she was setting up targets of rocks, cans, ration packages. Manning was always nearby, patiently explaining, chiding, congratulating. Though she recoiled at first when he put his arms around her to show her precise aiming procedure, how to overcome the AK-47's drift to the left, she gradually relaxed.

He taught her shoulder stance, snap-sighting, the full prone positions. She practiced rapid exchange of magazines by the hour; her switch-ins from safe to semiautomatic to full automatic became as natural as breathing; she could clear a jam with less than ten seconds down time.

The rest of the time she was content simply to hold her rifle in her lap, fingers moving over the polished stock, lightly fretting the trigger.

"Fucking spooky if you ask me," McCarter once commented, watching the display from a distance. He shuddered. "If she ever gets Blackwell in her sights...."

Manning, with his lifelong kinship with weapons of all sorts, was the best possible teacher. And she was an exemplary student. Within thirty-six hours' time she was holding a full thirty-round grouping in a three-square-foot perimeter—that at full automatic.

Her expression as she tore up the marked side of a deserted hut was demonic. Her lips were drawn into a snarl, her eyes glazed with hatred.

By the third day Nemtala had drawn almost completely from her shell; she turned into a glowing, beautiful woman. Returning Katz's baggy camouflage shirt, she replaced it with a tan top that fitted more snugly. She retained the shorts and the liberated boots.

Thrown together, Manning and Nemtala naturally developed a deep rapport. When they were not talking guns, there was slow exploration of backgrounds; Manning told her about the alien clime of Canada, Tala gave him extra insights into bedouin lore. There was time for talk of personal preferences and perceptions.

But these trusting confidences were for Manning alone. If another Phoenix Force member got too close, attempted to offer suggestions about her rifle-handling skills, Nemtala froze and flashed a defiant glare.

"If she was a cat she'd hiss," a rueful Encizo—who considered himself quite a hand with the ladies—commented after one such rebuff.

He and Katz had exchanged knowing glances. "Let them be," the Israeli had sighed.

Late that same afternoon all hands had good cause to be grateful for the added firepower Nemtala brought to their scruffy squad.

One moment they were slowly working their way up a steep, spine-jarring stretch of goat path, a blind passage ahead, the next the Libyan desert was blowing up in their faces.

Luckily they had paused to disconnect the FAV at the bottom of the incline to lessen the drain on the Land Rover, and the moment the first jarring crack of rifle fire was heard above and on the right—the whine of Kalashnikov slugs passing five feet overhead—Keio goosed the assault vehicle for all it was worth, slamming it to a stop on the low side of the LR. It was Encizo's turn on the MK-19, and with a growl he plummeted down onto the hood, scooted behind the MG, whipping off the dust canvas, yanking the cocking arm back in one fluid motion.

"Move out, *compadre*," he bellowed.

McCarter shoved the Land Rover into reverse and deliberately took a ditching to the right, snugging it to the sheer rock wall. The enemy would have to lean over the edge of the stone palisade to draw bead on them.

Manning followed McCarter's lead. The second the truck crunched to a halt, Manning, Tala and Salibogo bailed out, cartridge belts clamped, assault rifles freed up. They went straight west, intending to flank the base of the *jebel*, come around the blind side of the enemy.

"The bastards are out of range," Encizo shouted in stuttering outcry, Ohara's maneuverings all but throwing him from his station behind the MG. "That's why they aren't hitting anything."

"Hang on," Keio warned as he saw a yawning crater ahead. "Got a real sand pit here."

The FAV hit the rut, bounced three feet into the air, tilted dangerously, then landed on its left wheels. "God," Rafael groaned, as they came down on all four and jackrabbited forward. Ahead they caught a glimpse of a single Unimog, drawn into a shadowed cul-de-sac on the trail's right side. This time the terrorists had left a guard. As they rounded the low-slung butte, the Cobra gunner swung the Goryonov SG34 and opened up.

Back at the LR, Katz and McCarter hotfooted it along the base of the bluff, Soviet kisses raining down in a futile shower ten feet to their left. A richocheting 5.56mm slug chipped the rock wall near Yakov's head. Katz froze, craned his neck up the two-hundred-foot rise. He sent a burst of Uzi hellfire at the black head that was momentarily exposed.

They pushed on, pausing here and there to dump lead.

"I cannot believe this," Katz gasped, the Uzi chatterbox jerking in his fist. "That Blackwell would actually send out a second search party. Stupid. Apparently he doesn't believe in absorbing his losses." He snorted in disgust. "Even more stupid—we got caught flat-footed."

"These things happen, mate," McCarter encouraged. "They heard us before we heard them."

The two warriors broke and stopped, broke and stopped, making for the forward point where the FAV was just disappearing. Once Encizo had mopped up there, they had some tricky mountain climbing ahead of them.

Manning, Salibogo and Nemtala, meanwhile, were already starting up the backside of the desert citadel, digging feet and fingers into outcroppings, gruntingly drawing themselves up foot by foot. Manning was amazed at Salibogo's agility and endurance. He was aware of the vengeful expression twisting the faces of father and daughter, both oblivious to danger, the impending meeting with their mortal enemy blotting out everything else. Tala was actually outstripping Manning. When she glared back at them, her eyes strangely glazed, he snapped, "I go over first, Tala, understand? That's an order."

"Yes, Gary," she murmured in quick obedience. Again she was scrambling ahead.

Atop the Unimog the gunner was a heartbeat too slow in cranking up the Russian meat grinder. The FAV's unexpected, silent catapulting into his fire zone had seen to that. As the terrorist chambered the first round, the Mark 19 was already hammering skull-blasters home.

It only took one forty mill to do the job. All at once the man found his face missing.

His reflexes razor sharp, Keio did not even wait for the corpse to keel over, drop away from the mount. He rammed the attack wagon beyond the Unimog and sought protection deeper in the gorge. As he helped Encizo yank the Mark 19's stand-up mount to higher elevation, slammed the pintle home, Blackwell's goons were potting at them from overhead.

Then, moving on instinct alone, Keio was out of the FAV, zigzagging down the narrow valley, AK-47s pounding rivets into the gravel inches behind his heels. By then the MK-19 was at full bay, and the sky patrol went out of business momentarily.

As with all of Mack Bolan's men, Keio Ohara had received intensive indoctrination on every weapon known to Konzaki. Leaping into the Unimog, he took only twenty seconds to put the Russian MMG into action. Searching the rim of the cliff, he found a terrorist ranger silly enough to hang his nose out.

The bastard was shot dead with his own armament.

Keio and Rafael staked out sections of the stony parapet, panning the machine guns over the edge. The instant there was movement they opened up, chopping out big chunks of rocks, the splinter-hail brushing the terrorists back.

Minutes later more Marines landed, as McCarter and Katzenelenbogen stormed around the corner, sent a grateful high sign to their gun team. Without pause, they began clambering over a scrambled rockfall, heading for the high country. Their ascent was easy— the blocks provided good footing, and the angle was steep but not impossible.

Blackwell's men did not even know an assault team was on the way; Keio and Rafael saw to it that reconnaissance was kept at absolute minimum. Now Yakov and McCarter were halfway up the cliff. Thirty feet. Fifteen feet. Then, hovering just under the lip, they were locked and bolted, waiting for Encizo to lob a half dozen grenade cartridges.

There was a sudden change in tactics. For at that moment the muted, metallic clatter of rapid fire carried from farther back on the table top outpost. Manning and company.

Yakov motioned Keio and Rafael to hold their fire and started slowly working his way upward. "A foot at a time," he said, straining as his prosthetic hook caught in a slight outcrop, drew him upward. "Quick roll at full fire when we go over."

Up on the battleground, the remaining Black Cobras were in full panic. One of the twelve-man team was dead, an oozing hole in the side of his head; another was seriously wounded, rolling in agony where a Goryonov slug had punched out most of his shoulder.

The rear guard, distracted by the awesome thunder of the Mark 19, were caught unprepared. Before they could react to the blazingly swift appearance of the three commandos, to the blurring sweep on the right, left and front, they were goners. The invaders fell flat on the stony apron to the west. Their rifles caught fire, hosing terrorists with slashing lead.

A tall white man, an old man and a girl—this was the extent of the image emblazoned on their retinas in that instant just before their lights went out forever.

During the firefight, Manning, in a fleeting glance took in Tala's performance. She was dedicated, professional, entirely fearless. He was awed by this female killing machine, which he had helped create.

Her face formed a demonic grimace. She moved the AK-47 in precise, smooth sweeps, plucking off separate bursts, bringing down one man, moving to the next with no wasted motions—or bullets—whatsoever. Before the deafening clatter died down, she alone was responsible for five of the corpses littering the land.

It was all over. As suddenly as the stunning fight had started, it died out. Faces grim, slumped in washout pose, their weapons pointing slackly toward the ground, the ragtag trio surveyed the havoc they had made.

Shortly there was a call from Yakov. "Is it all right to come up? All clear, Manning?"

"All clear," he said, his voice empty.

Colonel Yakov Katzenelenbogen muttered as he took in the blood-drenched scene.

"No survivors, I suppose," Katz finally said.

Manning shrugged. "We can check around."

They walked among the eleven men slowly, Yakov turning one over with his boot, then another. And when they came to the shoulder-mangled trooper Keio was responsible for. . . .

"Spare me, effendi," he gasped, his voice barely audible. "Show mercy, I. . . ."

The words went unfinished. Nemtala strode forward and aimed a vicious kick at his head. The man groaned harshly, rolled partially away. "Just like the mercy you showed the people of Abu Darash?" she rasped in matching dialect. "Answer my captain's questions or die like the camel dung you are."

Manning drew Nemtala away.

"Where is General Blackwell?" Yakov demanded. "Where is he heading?" Salibogo translated.

"Three days we have traveled," the Cobra gasped, "to find our missing comrades. When last I saw him he was in Ba Debba. The main force moved out that same night."

Katz frowned as Salibogo translated the man's last statement. "Ask him where Blackwell's heading," he snapped.

"I am a mere foot soldier," the man replied, cringing before the Israeli's hard stare. "I am told nothing. I go where they tell me to go. A poor foot soldier, I tell you."

As Salibogo relayed the reply, his daughter again intruded. "Tell my captain what he wants to know, scum," she grated, jamming the barrel of her AK-47 into his face. The man tried to evade her, but she slammed her boot onto his shredded shoulder, forced him back. And before anyone could stop her, the rifle barrel slashed harder, taking out most of his teeth. "Talk, you animal."

"Nemtala," Katz said, his eyes dark with rage.

But the woman, out of touch at the moment, seemingly did not hear, and again the gun barrel was poised for a fresh smash at his mouth.

"I am only a soldier," the man jabbered more desperately, spitting teeth in growing terror, expending the last of his strength. "I swear, I do not know any of these things you ask. I swear, on my mother's grave."

"Well," Nemtala sniffed, "you are of no further use to us then, are you?" In that moment her AK-47 discharged a single bullet, creating a hole in his forehead.

A stunning silence enveloped them then, all eyes wide at the bizarre turn.

Nemtala seemed to break from a trance, then she recoiled, stared confusedly down at the mess she had made of the Cobra's head—a sickening sight.

She flung herself away, ran to the edge of the precipice and stared over. Manning was instantly behind her, his hands bracing her shoulders. She fell to her knees and began to sob bitterly. A moment later she was vomiting into the sand. Manning knelt beside her, offered her his handkerchief when she was done.

Nemtala turned and buried her face in his shoulder. "What is happening?" she choked. "Why am I doing these things? I am becoming animal. More animal than the man we are after. Oh, Gary, Gary...."

The others turned away as Manning tried desperately to comfort her.

They watched with quiet amusement as Salibogo again began stripping weapons from the fallen hardmen, adding them to the lot already in their Unimog. "I swear, he'll be selling guns to Blackwell before he's through," Encizo said.

The Goryonov SG34 was also loaded—beside its twin—in Phoenix's rolling armory. Again fuel was transferred between the various vehicles, precious water supply was replenished.

"Good old Blackwell," Keio mused. "Who needs a quartermaster section with him around?"

They did not fire the abandoned Unimog this time. Instead they dropped a grenade into the engine, blasted away the tires. It was left to rot. A century from now—the Libyan desert being the arid, rainless hellbox it was—the vehicle would still be there, bogged in the sand.

They headed out at 1900 hours. They would drive all night long. Blackwell was a burr beneath Katzenelenbogen's saddle by now; Katz would make up for lost time the best way he could. And if it meant driving Phoenix Force to the limit....

They headed due east, the African sun a ruddy orange fireball slowly sinking at their backs.

9

By noon of the next day, the men of Phoenix Force had come to the end of their string. Even though they had taken turns spelling each other with the driving throughout the long, cold night, the exertions of the past week finally took their toll. Katzenelenbogen—though haunted by a gnawing sense of urgency—finally called a halt. He was sure the marathon drive had cut another day off Blackwell's lead.

Their lucky discovery of the heavenlike oasis of Wadi el-Tonjo contributed in part to his decision.

What better spot for brief R&R?

Wadi el-Tonjo was not a spectacular oasis, but to the parched, dirty, reeking men of Phoenix it was nothing short of a godsend. After a week of unrelenting wasteland, the greenery of the place was paradise. The ground springs, even though it was late April, had not dried up. The small pool, brackish yet clear, was perhaps twenty by twenty and reached a depth of four feet at its center. Three palms, a sparse grove of thorn trees, plus reeds and bunch grass around the pool proper, assumed proportions of dense forest to the sand-blitzed crew.

They were not alone at the oasis. A nomad tribe consisting of six men, eight women and twelve children along with two camels and a herd of scrawny sheep had arrived there.

No words were exchanged, except by Salibogo and the family headman, and upon seeing the heavy guns the foreigners carried, the natives kept wary distance. They cooked, stayed near their ragged tents, saw to filling numerous goatskin bags with water from the spring.

Respecting the water rights, Phoenix did not plunge headfirst into the shallow pool, as McCarter had boisterously proposed. Instead pails of water were drawn, heated, carried behind a hastily erected canvas screen. Here—luxury of luxuries—the men had scrubbed down, washed their hair, shaved and generally wallowed in the novelty of being clean again.

When they had finished with their GI party, moved about in fresh clothes, Nemtala, still shamefaced over yesterday's lapse, had appeared and gone behind the tarp-rigged screen. When she emerged a half hour later, she was amazingly transformed. Wearing a white *taub*, her long hair glistening, this feminine charmer seemed unconnected to the bloodthirsty fanatic who had fought shoulder-to-shoulder with them only hours before.

They then had a leisurely meal, the C rations tasting almost like food in their festive mood. Katz produced a bottle of Scotch from his duffel and passed it from man to man.

Their sense of oneness was very high just then.

The meal went on. The bottle went around a second, then a third time. It was McCarter who killed it. Grinning foolishly, he rose. "Now where's that damned camel I'm supposed to kiss?" he quipped.

Throughout the meal everyone noticed that Nemtala sat very close to Manning, a new, almost proprietary glow in her gaze.

What remained of the afternoon was given over to housekeeping chores. Clothes were scrubbed, put out to dry. Weapons were cleaned, vehicles received key-point maintenance. Ammo was inventoried, made more readily accessible because the specter of swiftly approaching showdown was much with them.

But mostly—sleep.

Bedrolls were flopped in every shady spot. Men collapsed into hard, strength-replenishing sleep.

Modesty still strong within her, Nemtala returned to the Unimog, spread her bedding in its shade. Her need for emotional and physical recharge vastly eclipsed theirs.

Only Salibogo—accepting unspoken responsibility—did not sleep. Huddled in the shade of a solitary desert mango tree, his AK-47 close at hand, he kept watch.

There was a late supper at 1900 hours. Early bed-check, Katz insisted. They would be up before dawn. They *would* make up for lost time. Each man would take a turn at watch duty.

"Sleep fast," he quipped with a dry smile.

Encizo, Ohara, Manning and Nemtala sat up an hour longer once the sun had dropped off the horizon. A small fire burned in the middle of the staging area as they sat cross-legged in the sand, staring into the flames. The night chill built swiftly.

The tiny berries on the thorn tree twigs popped noisily in the fire, sending up a miniature display of phosphorescent fireworks. The soft fireglow gave Nemtala's eyes a sensuous, provocative sheen, enhanced her exotic beauty. Her face impassive, her thoughts distant, unreadable, she was again close to Manning. Her growing shadow status did not go unnoticed. Nor did the recent change in Manning. Deep, disturbing thoughts were at large behind his gray eyes as well.

Encizo nudged Ohara, shot a quick look to Manning and Nemtala. "The top's gonna boil off that soon," he whispered. "Damned soon."

Keio smiled thoughtfully, nodded.

Shortly Rafael drew his stocky frame to full height, shouldered his Stoner. "Better start walking my post," he said.

"I'll be turning in, too, I guess," Keio said.

Reluctantly, Manning untangled his long legs. "Goodnight, Tala," he muttered awkwardly, looking back once before he set out for his sleeping bag, spread in a semiisolated gully in the sand, roughly a hundred fifty feet from the Land Rover.

"Good night, Gary," she sighed, a winsome curve to her lips. "I. . . ."

"Tala?"

"Good night." She turned, went toward the Unimog, her movements somehow laggard, regretful. She faded into the gloom.

Encizo did not really intend to patrol the perimeter of their bivouac. Instead he found a dark vantage point between their camp and that of the nomads. Planting his back against a palm tree, balancing the Stoner across his legs, he was ready for anything.

He was in a good spot to see the blurred motion off beyond the Unimog—the white-robed phantom that fled along the edge of the dunes, moved in faltering strides toward the place where Gary Manning was bedded down. A thin, wise smile crossed his face. An envious smile.

Manning heard the soft swish of sand off to the right and instinctively came alert, his hand closing on his H&K. His scalp prickled as he recognized the voice. "Do not shoot, Gary," it whispered. "It is me. Tala."

A moment later she was standing over him, staring down with wide, beseeching eyes. In the eerie half light she deftly undid the sash of her *taub*, let the cotton garment float to her feet. His eyes widened in disbelief as he saw her exquisite nakedness, the glowing, proud breasts, the slim legs, the voluptuous flare of hips.

With a rush she was beside him, groping for the zipper of his sleeping bag. Manning tore it down, dazedly slid aside to give her room.

"Gary," she giggled nervously, shivering, her lips inches from his, her eyes glistening with luminous mischief. "Do you want me?" The question was essence of total, childlike naiveté. "Do you want me...as woman? *I* want you."

Something shattered inside his chest, and his voice snagged. "Yes, Tala," he choked. "I do."

He put his arms around her, the warmth and smoothness of her skin electrifying under his fingertips. He drew her close, buried his lips in the side of her silky, fragrant throat. "You lovely, beautiful darling..." Manning whispered.

She withdrew, stared down again, her gaze liquid.
"Is that a love word? Darling?"

"Yes."

"Then I call you darling. Gary. . . darling."

He could not believe this was happening; he was
sure he must be dreaming, that he would shortly
awake. But as his hands slid restlessly up and down her
tawny back, as he felt the thrust of her passion-
hardened nipples against his chest, as he felt the shud-
der of her lower body against his, he conceded that it
was no dream.

She accepted him, welcomed him. As lover, as pro-
tector, as teacher, as friend.

His kiss was gentle, searching, intoxicating. He
touched her tentatively, slowly.

Tala hissed, arched her body. How, she pondered,
her body tensing in exquisite pleasure, could this man,
a warrior so fierce in battle, be so sweetly considerate,
so mild.

His touch was velvety, adoring. This was man, this
was love in every glorious sense of the word. She
flowered inside, felt herself sink more deeply into a
drowsy, delicious state.

"Oh, darling," she said, testing the term, the only
love word she knew. "My darling. . . ."

10

The Black Cobra army was in bivouac in an end-of-the-world wadi approximately twelve miles east of Abu Hamed. Massive camouflage nets spread over the cluster of Unimogs, trucks and command cars provided relative shade for the two-hundred-sixty-odd troops sprawled everywhere, recuperating from their last eighty-mile run.

Though it was 0100 hours, and Blackwell should have been sleeping, the Cobra leader felt sleep was out the question just then.

Alternately pacing the gravelly sand of the Nubian desert and hanging over the shoulder of Attilo Malwal, the officer responsible for their communications net, he was beside himself with rage. Not only were they behind schedule in their march to the sea, but there was the more nagging problem of the two missing search parties he had sent after that blasted bedouin tramp.

Lieutenant Malwal was not having any more success getting something out of his alleged radioman than Blackwell had. Hovering over the shortwave radio in what had been Ochogilo's command car, General Blackwell ground his teeth in frustration.

"Nothing, sir," Malwal said, raising his hands in

apologetic gesture. "We cannot raise anybody in Munzoga. No one is manning the radio, apparently."

"Lazy bastards," Blackwell stormed. "They should have checked in by now. What in hell are we paying them so-called counteragents for?"

He pushed back his elaborate dress cap, the bill emblazoned with outrageous tangle of gold braid, and stared up at the mottled camo net. "Where in hell did them bastards get to?" he said to nobody in particular. "One of the squads should be reporting back by now."

The tall, almost emaciated black, his cheekbones gaunt, his eyes haunted, commenced his impatient loping again. His lips moved nonstop while he contemplated.

And suppose those men did not come back, he speculated. What could it mean? Did they get lost in the desert? Highly unlikely. Aboud and Nyamahanga were good men; they had been with him from the earliest days.

What, then? Desert? Hell, no. They were as high on the program as he was. They were in to the bitter end.

Native resistance? That set-to in Al-Rashad, maybe? An ambush by the locals? Hardly. They didn't know one end of a rifle from the other. Scratch that notion.

Suffocatingly hot as it was under the netting, Blackwell was nevertheless whipped by a sudden chill. He stopped in midstride. Was there someone out there? Another attack force? The Chad outfit? Coming after him?

He shrugged that one off, too. Who, then? Who had the firepower, the knowhow to knock out three dozen of his best men? The chill grew stronger, pierced to the marrow of his bones. He could let nothing, no one stop him now—not when he was so close to achieving his pivotal mission, that first big step. Bring this one in, and he was halfway home.

The CIA, he mused. Could it be? They were always poking their noses where they were not wanted. Had the supersnoops somehow got wind of his plan? Had they enlisted a gang of mercs, put them on his tail? God knows there was no shortage of guns-for-hire in Africa these days.

Blackwell shook off the thoughts. Can't be. No way. We'll be hearing soon. A breakdown, that's what it was. They'll show up before the day's out. They'll check with the Munzoga network, get our bearings, head on in.

But Blackwell was not entirely reassured. He continued his restless pacing, his brow more deeply furrowed than before.

AT THAT MOMENT, at Aswan, roughly three hundred miles to the north, atop the parapet of the High Dam, Yuri Kirov, a highly placed KGB gopher presently attached to a Russian terrorist branch known as Department V, was slowly promenading on the visitors' view point, along with sidekick Alexei Yevgeny.

Posing as tourists, carrying cameras and binoculars, both talked in muffled voices, planning a bloody bath for the people of Egypt.

Colonel Kirov was no stranger to the High Dam. He had been one of the top Soviet engineers assigned to the supervision of its construction, which began in

1960, and he had remained there until 1972, when Sadat had kicked the entire Russian delegation out of the country.

Memory of that humiliation rankled to this day. Thus, when General Donvyov, commandant of Department V, had summoned him and outlined the crucial mission, Kirov had been only too happy to accept. Deliriously happy. Vengeance—long-delayed vengeance—is always sweet.

Standing apart from a guided tour that was passing, Kirov spoke rapid-fire Russian. "Perhaps there was no real need for me to come here," he said. "After all, I know the dam like the back of my hand. But if one is planning a surprise such as ours...it doesn't hurt to double-check."

He pointed to the vast blockhouse to his right, on the Aswan Dam's northern face, then to the intake gate almost directly opposite, on the southern side, where the waters of Lake Nasser glittered blindingly in the sun. "This is where the rocket will strike," he said. "It would be useless to attack the high walls. It would take a five-megaton warhead to blow the dam itself.

"As it is, the one missile will do nicely." He looked at the power-plant complex, where the twelve turbo-electric generators, producing ten billion kilowatt hours annually, were located. "We will kill two birds with one missile."

The intake-gate crane and all six tunnels, Kirov said, detailing the destruction strategy, would take the main brunt of the blast. With every gate open and the means of closing them blown to kingdom come, the three hundred miles of water backed up into northern Egypt and southern Sudan would be given free rein. At first the deluge would be minor. But as the millions of cubic feet of water impacted in savage, relentless pressure, the tunnels would crumble. The widening would increase the speed of the torrent even more.

"Within forty-eight hours," Major Kirov gloated, "the intake area will totally disintegrate. The entire wall there will collapse. And there goes Egypt. Sudan as well."

"Beautiful, Major," Yevgeny congratulated. "And the most beautiful part of it is that once the chain reaction starts, there is absolutely nothing they can do about it. Imagine the panic, the total frustration."

"By then the fall of the Egyptian government will be assured. It would take them six years to repair the damage. No, comrade, the dam will never be rebuilt. Not in our lifetime."

Both men fell silent as they continued to stare out at the vast expanse of Lake Nasser—three hundred sixty-five feet at its deepest point—where it shone in the ever-widening reservoir beyond the ridges of the Nugrus Highlands. Glazed, anticipatory light in their eyes, they felt an all-consuming pride at the ingenious simplicity of their plan.

Ingenious because when all was said and done, no blame would ever be attributed to the Soviet Union. All responsibility for the horrendous catastrophe would fall on that black madman, General Jeremiah Blackwell. The Soviet Union and Cuba would emerge with lily-white hands.

A nation, a civilization would be utterly destroyed; the precarious balance of the Middle East would teeter into chaos. All existing political alliances would be undermined. And the U.S., France, England, Israel, Germany could do absolutely nothing about it.

The two Russians finally emerged from their smug trance and began to walk along the esplanade of the three-mile-long dam. They paused to take some photographs with an ultralong lens and jotted precise notes on distances, angles of trajectory. Visual estimates were second nature to Colonel Kirov.

"Come," the engineer said forty minutes later, "we have sufficient data. Let us return to our hotel. A few vodkas, Alexei? A good day's work. We have earned it."

ANOTHER GOOD DAY'S WORK was also being concluded in the Red Sea port city of Beylul, located in Ethiopia, just across the Bay of Mandeb from South Yemen. It was dusk, and under cover of a humid fog, the *Iraqu III*, a medium-size freighter of undetermined registry, was being loaded with one of the most vital elements in the Aswan strategy.

The missile was of U.S. origin—a thirty-four-foot-long Nike Ajax—and along with its improvised carrier launcher, it was giving the *Iraqu*'s crewmen fits. Had they known the missile was loaded with a one-megaton nuclear warhead capable of blowing its way through fifty feet of solid concrete, they might have fled the decks of the decrepit vessel in screaming terror.

Watching from dockside, Captain Angel DeRosa smiled broadly. His part of the mission was on deadline; the rest of it was up to Blackwell. And to Sadiq

Des Fara-Lit, fanatical leader of the Eritrean People's Liberation Front, who would give his right arm to overthrow Sudan's president, Jaafar al-Nemery. It was Fara-Lit who had volunteered to back up the Black Cobra forces should the need arise.

Sometimes, though he considered himself a professional terrorist, DeRosa got a headache trying to keep the conniving terrorist factions in this part of Africa—Ethiopia, Sudan, Yemen—separate.

It was from Yemen that the Nike Ajax had originated. Where had the Commies got it? For an answer there was much shrugging, but no definite info. The closest the Cuban liaison-organizer specialist had got to explanation was that it had been salvaged from a U.S. cruiser that had "mysteriously" gone down in the Gulf of Aden. The CIA was still fuming over this minor coup.

The missile had been gone over and completely rebuilt by Soviet experts; most certainly it was now totally operational.

DeRosa watched the long thin crate being safely bedded into a thick mat of straw. As he saw the mechanized carrier finally crane-lowered into the *Iraqu*'s hold, he breathed a fervent sigh of relief. Now he could get back to his black stooge, Jeremiah Blackwell, and keep him on track. The stupid episode with that Arab *puta*, the resultant search parties, had been particularly distressful to him.

"Eh, bueno," he said to Lieutenant Alcero Quintero, *his* liaison between South Yemen and Sadiq Des Fara-Lit and al-Mahdi. "At last. I thought those fools would never get the equipment loaded."

DeRosa handed Quintero a bulky, brown envelope. Unmarked, but plainly containing a great wad of currency.

"I have kept my end of the bargain, Quintero," he grumped. "I trust that you will keep yours."

"Exactamente, mi capitán," the junior officer assured. "Fara-Lit has been informed. His troops are on standby status. The captain of the *Iraqu* has his instructions. The cargo will be offloaded at Halaib within three days, where, as I understand it, Rejection Front people will enter the picture, see to moving it into Egypt, within range of the Aswan. Your Blackwell will provide guard, will see to the actual firing of the missile. We want none of that—" he made a distasteful grimace "—on our heads."

Qunitero rubbed his hands. "Should there be anything left of the missile. . . any incriminating shreds whatsoever. . . guess who shall be fixed with the blame?"

Shortly Quintero bid his partner in terror adieu, melted into the gathering gloom. DeRosa stayed on the dock another half hour, waiting until he saw the *Iraqu* cast off and begin its sluggish northward run into the Red Sea.

APPROXIMATELY ONE THOUSAND MILES to the northwest, an eighteen-hour run behind them, the men of Phoenix Force were settling into a hard, replenishing sleep. The next day they would hit the relative metropolis of Munzoga, where, they hoped, crucial linkup with Stony Man's top-secret African network would be made. If anyone knew where Blackwell was, could provide pinpoint coordinates, these dedicated counter-agents could. But for tonight—sleep.

In one isolated outpost of the hasty bivouac, no sleeping was going on; it was the farthest thing from Gary Manning's mind.

Again Tala had magically appeared from the all-suffocating darkness. Again, freshly washed and fragrant, she had invaded her lover's sleeping bag. Again they were naked, body to body, lips locked, hands feverishly caressing and exploring.

Their bodies twined, locked, began ecstatic crash and recoil. Their murmurings, whispers climbed.

"*Ana bahibek,*" Tala choked. "Oh, Gary. It is so. I do love you."

And though Manning did not want to commit himself, though he was not ready at this early point in time to admit his sudden dependence upon this incredible female, he was helpless before the hurricane of emotion within his heart at that moment.

"Tala," he groaned, "I love you."

Tala buried her mouth in his shoulder, stifled her scream of primal delight, felt her heart expand to joyful near-bursting.

Afterward, as their bodies were still, as their breathing evened out, she began to sob against him. The woman was learning—love has its price. It can be very sweet indeed—a paradise of delight and happiness.

But it can also be unspeakably sad.

11

Phoenix Force caught first sight of the hazy smear of smog over Munzoga at 1615 hours. The city of perhaps twenty thousand people was still an hour away. Primitive by modern-day standards, Munzoga assumed Big Apple status to the civilization-starved commandos. Though all knew the layover's real purpose, a holiday buzz still jangled mental circuits.

Katzenelenbogen called a halt perhaps six miles due north of Munzoga. Closing on the Nubian desert, the terrain taking on definite new cragginess, they holed up in a protected gully between forty-foot-high ridges of rock.

Tomorrow, early, there would be time for restocking of fuel and water. But for now—water to waste. Shave, scrub down. Also, a fresh change of clothing, sand brushed from boots.

Phoenix Force decided nighttime entry to the city would be best; the less attention they attracted, the better. The murky desert darkness would prove a good ally as they skulked the narrow, winding streets, seeking to locate the undercover contacts that Brognola and April Rose had provided that last afternoon at Stony Man. Only two weeks ago? It seemed a year had passed.

They would enter in the Land Rover. It would be unwise to roll in with assault rifles and machine guns in full view. Somebody would have to remain behind. Coins had been flipped. And flipped again. A very disgruntled Keio Ohara became the watchdog.

It was imperative that Salibogo and Nemtala accompany the recon force. Their skills as interpreters, their ability to warn of hostile vibrations would prove invaluable once inside the alien camp. And how would they ever find the street called Sharia Ali Unqulah in a tangled maze this size?

It was 2000 hours, dusk finally having given way to a mineshaft darkness, when they picked their way out of the desert.

Phoenix Force rolled into Munzoga. The low, square-cut structures, here and there a mosque spire or a pasha's residence, poked above the matchbox construction. In the murk the hundreds of miles of walls, crazily winding and doubling-back streets became an impenetrable labyrinth.

Feeble electric lights shone in erratic sequence, the spaces in between becoming black, treacherous no-man's-land. The sand roads—barely wide enough to accommodate one vehicle—were rutted and potholed, demanding low gear. The farther they got into the city, the more overpowering became the maze effect. The endless array of high mud walls—painted in washed-out shades of gray, white and tan—hyped claustrophobic tendencies.

Behind the walls they saw half-domed peaks of more affluent residences; shafts of cypress, acacia, date palms, even a baobab tree, climbed against the night sky.

Most of the homes were already dark, but sporadic flickers from candles and oil lamps could be seen. A bare light bulb—the mark of wealthy family—cut the blackness with near-blinding brilliance.

Gradually, up ahead, things grew brighter; they were approaching the city's center. Here Munzoga's bazaars, restaurants, public buildings and business offices proudly flaunted their modernity.

"What a hole," Encizo groused, his words garbled by the joltings of the corrugated roadbed. "And I was hoping to find a classy nightclub somewhere, dance the night away with the girl of my dreams."

The Land Rover lurched viciously as it made a corner, turned into Munzoga's main square. The buildings were taller, laid out on grander scale. Hundreds of people sat in chairs, benches, around outside coffeehouse tables, enjoying the oncoming coolness. More people walked around the edges of the vast square.

Vehicles were parked helter-skelter along what passed for curbside in the plaza, most of them vintage items, dating back fifteen, twenty years. The Land Rover's appearance caused a stir, and necks craned everywhere for better view of the outsiders.

Among those citizens with an instinctive feel for trouble, eyes instantly narrowed, expressions became guarded. These night loungers had seen mercenaries before; if these men were not hired guns, then they were the next best thing to it.

Katz and Salibogo climbed from the LR and began a slow walk around the square. Seeing a moderately friendly and curious face, they walked over, paused at the coffee-house table. A long rigmarole of Arabic amenities between Salibogo and the edgy townsmen ensued.

Finally Salibogo asked if the gentlemen would be kind enough to direct them to Sharia Ali Unqulah?

There was an immediate shadowing in the eyes, an unmistakable pause. It was apparent that the address was well-known. And who did they want to find on that street?

Salibogo courteously informed them that it was none of their business. The citizens shrugged, smiled, began a long, detailed explanation of how many corners, how many stock corrals, how many date palms they must pass before they found the street.

Munzoga was well-known as a hotbed of political intrigue. The Libyans, the Eritreans, the Chaddites, the Ansar all had listening posts here. These latest outlanders were but a few in an endless parade of insurgents and counterinsurgents; state coups were arranged on a daily basis.

Thus, it was not unexpected that the Phoenix Force feelers would draw covert attention from adjoining tables; indeed, there were several passersby who matter-of-factly sidled up, ears on strings. And as the elaborate instructions peeled off yard upon yard, one of these eavesdroppers, unnoticed by Katz or Salibogo, furtively eased away from his table, faded into the night.

Finally, after a dozen more salaams and *Ba'allah*s, they parted company with their new friends and hurried back to the Land Rover.

Finding Sharia Ali Unqulah consumed another forty-five minutes. In the darkness and the mouse-tunnel streets, they got lost twice, and again they had to talk with drowsy-eyed locals who reluctantly answered from behind locked doors. And if Phoenix had been counting on any kind of clandestine appointment—forget it.

They might as well have put an ad in the paper.

At long last, at 2200 hours, before a high-walled structure, they saw a barely discernible Ibrahim scrawled on the plank gate. *"Aywa?"* the soft voice called from behind the palisade. "Who is there? How may I serve you?"

"Abdel Ibrahim?" Katzenelenbogen responded.

"Yes?"

"El-khabr esh-shum yusal bi-l-agal," Katz said, his mouth close to the gate. Bad news arrives with speed— the curious password provided by Stony Man.

Thirty seconds later, a series of chains and crossbars falling behind the door, they were swiftly ushered inside. All except Gary Manning. "You watch the car," Yakov ordered. "We won't be long."

Nemtala hung back, intending to stay with Manning.

"No," Katz intervened. "You come with us, Nemtala. This may get sticky. We're going to need all the help we can get with this guy."

Still she was torn, her eyes darting between her lover and her accepted commanding officer. She wheeled and followed the rest of them inside the gate, which was quickly rebarred by a small, lithe man of about fifty.

"You have come at last," he said in mishmash of English and Arabic. "I have give you up for lost."

He led them through a small courtyard. Everything was immaculate. Even the sand around the plantings and surrounding the single date palm had been recently swept and graded.

Inside, the mud walls were enameled in a dark blue motif, the furnishings expensive and modern. After the darkness in the streets, the electric lamps were glaring. Obviously Ibrahim was a well-paid counteragent.

Katzenelenbogen declined Ibrahim's offer of coffee and something to eat. Business came first.

"Yes, of course," Ibrahim nodded. "The information." All noted he was careful not to ask for or to mention their names or those of his employer—the mark of a truly professional intelligence man. "I have everything you could possibly want on our black friend."

"He has been this way?"

"Definitely. I have dates, times, coordinates. He is less than thirty-six hours away." Ibrahim smiled proudly. "I even have network in Munzoga pinpointed. Should you care to close that shop down before you leave."

For the next twenty minutes the conversation was quick, detailed; it stalled only when the language barrier became formidable. As it turned out the Phoenix headman's decision to keep Nemtala close at hand paid off; many of Ibrahim's technical references sailed clean over Salibogo's head.

"A missile strike?" Katz sucked in a harsh, disbelieving gasp. "Are you sure? How did you find that out?"

"Yes, I am sure," Ibrahim said. "I have ways of

finding out these things. Your people in America pay for best. They get best.''

Katzenelenbogen's head spun wildly. A missile? Dispatched from anywhere within a twenty- to two-hundred-mile radius of the High Dam? How in hell were they supposed to find that in time? Scrap Brognola's radio silence. They would have to make contact somehow, call in extra firepower. They were damned well out of their depth with a land mission.

The briefing went on. The spy provided charts, pinpointed the last known location of the Black Cobras, speculated on their route of march. He gave fleeting fill on which groups might possibly be involved in the complicated plot.

"This local outfit?" Katz drilled in, "the Eritreans? The ELF? Their hideout in Munzoga.... Can you finger them?"

Again the man puffed up. Modesty was certainly not his strongest suit. "But of course, effendi. Nothing on paper, understand, but I am reasonably positive who the main contact is. A man named...."

Abdel Ibrahim's last bit of puffery proved his undoing. And that of Phoenix Force. For at that moment they all froze, shooting frantic looks at the high, domed ceiling. A rapid scuttling of footsteps carried from overhead.

As the counteragent darted right, attempted to slap off the main light switch, the crash of splintering glass was heard. Then a triple-tongued burst of machine-pistol fire exploded in the close confines of the room. Abdel went down in a grunting heap, the front of his white *galabieh* suddenly saturated with blood.

His eyes went wide with disbelief, rolled for a last time. Dedicated professional to the end, he fought to spit out the contact's name to Katz. But the words were drowned in a gush of blood that suddenly issued from his mouth.

Encizo hit the light switch and flung himself to the floor in one fluid movement. The room was instantly plunged into blackness; leather hissed in every corner of the room. Katz's Beretta 92-S, McCarter's Browning Hi Power 9mm both blasted up at the overhead bay, taking out the overconfident assassin.

When they heard him tumble down the dome, bounce on the roof, they were up, spreading out. Since all exits had been pinpointed the moment they had entered Ibrahim's home, Rafael kicked out a smallish window encased in a foot-thick arch in the wall facing the courtyard. McCarter broke for the rear of the house, shouldered open the door there. Katz undid the lock on the front door and used a chair to push it open. All dropped back, waiting for the chatter of automatic weapons. When only Yakov found a buyer—the characteristic sound of an AK-47 splitting the night—Rafael and McCarter bailed out, their automatics punching death. They hit the ground, swept a practiced recon, caught one ELF drone flat-footed as he sprinted straight back at them.

Rafael's Walther PPK spit .380 cal, ventilating the man's groin, while McCarter's nine mills slugged his chest with the impact of a linebacker's tackle. The bedouin bungler went down.

There was no time for a finish-off round. Their attention was caught by the thump and slap of sandaled feet along the courtyard's west wall. There, clinging to ropes thrown over the parapet, two men were walking up the sheer face like trained monkeys.

The Browning and Walther spun out a single round, each Phoenix sharpshooter tagging his man low in the spine, the upward trajectory of the slug churning a huge, gut-mangling hole through each terrorist goon.

The terrorists suddenly lost all interest in mountain climbing. They plummeted fifteen feet to the sand.

Rafael and McCarter crashed forward, eager for a desperate, last-minute game of twenty questions. But they were distracted. At the far end of the garden, through the main gate, which now hung wide open, they saw a fleeting shadow as Katz went in pursuit of yet another hardman. Instantly they were up and after him.

Their backup efforts were wasted. The Beretta poised, Katz zeroed on the waddling yards of white robe, squeezed off three fast rounds of 9mm.

The hit man raised his arms, spun almost completely around before he slammed facedown in the street.

He was still breathing when they reached him, and there was fleeting hope that they could still wring crucial info from him. Again they were cheated. The ELF patriot had drawn a long-bladed dagger, and now, as they rolled him over, he was defiantly burrowing it into his paunchy gut.

It was then, for the first time—all perspective lost in the midst of the chaotic, time-stopping action—that they realized . . . .

Where in hell was Manning?

Blood drained from their faces, the crushing sense of fear akin to taking a sudden haymaker in the belly.

"Oh, Jesus," McCarter gasped. "Gary. Them filthy bastards got Gary."

They stood in stunned disbelief, eyes darting to Ibrahim's gate, to the Land Rover, to the narrow, twisting street beyond.

But no Gary Manning.

"They must have blindsided him," Rafael murmured, his face a study in rage, frustration and dejection.

Cursing, McCarter blasted back into the courtyard, approached the two men at the base of the wall. One of them had to be alive. Both were dead.

Nemtala and Salibogo, unarmed, burst from the house. "Gary," Nemtala yelled, instinctively appraising the situation. She ran to the Land Rover, stared wildly inside.

Her despair was short-lived. Instinct told her that panic would not bring her lover back. A flitting dark shadow, she fell back into the courtyard. When she reappeared she had a Kalashnikov assault rifle over her shoulder, a cartridge belt in place. Another AK-47 hung in her free hand. This weapon she handed to her father. No tears. Only murder, cold and deadly, shone in her eyes.

"Bitching bloody hell," McCarter groaned, truly beside himself. "What do we do now?" He stared into the black, endless maze of streets. "Where do we begin to look in a dung heap like this?"

12

It was then, sound carrying incredible distances in the arid desert air, that they heard the faint whine of a vehicle off toward the west. The vehicle gradually wound through the gears and picked up speed.

"That's gotta be them," McCarter said, digging into his pocket for the Land Rover keys. "Who else'd be out driving at this time of night?" He plunged into the LR, kicked the engine to life. "Move it, you guys."

"Hang on," Encizo muttered, sprinting back to the courtyard. "I'm gonna even me some odds."

Quickly he returned, a third AK-47 in tow. And as he piled into the back, he handed a sheaf of papers to Katz. "Just an afterthought," he said. "These might come in handy."

Katz nodded gratefully. In his distress over Manning, he had forgotten the contact's papers.

The Land Rover bucked forward, McCarter howling in frustrated fury, curses rolling off his tongue in steady flow.

But they might as well have parked the vehicle.

Blind alley turned into blind alley. Time and time again, relying on instinct, following the drone of the far-off vehicle, they came up against a mocking wall.

Then it was bucking, roaring reverse, a flurry of wheel-spinnings to get the overland vehicle about-faced. And all the while precious minutes were getting away from them, the terrorist vehicle's noise becoming more faint by the moment.

Ten minutes later they found themselves back at Abdel Ibrahim's house.

"What now?" Encizo asked, putting voice to his panic. "This is crazy. We have no idea which way to turn in this maze. They could be holding Gary fifty yards away from where we're sitting. Or five miles. *Cristo*, if Abrahim had hung in there thirty seconds longer...."

For long, teeth-grinding moments they sat in silent funk. Katz, knowing he was responsible for decisions at such moments, was driven to the brink of brain-exploding despair.

It was Nemtala who suggested the only reasonable course of action. "We go back into city square," she said. "We ask people...anyone...if they know of Eritrean sympathizers." Her eyes flared desperately. "What else do we have?"

Katz paused a half minute more, then nodded. "She's right," he said. "God knows, we've got to start somewhere. We can't just sit here and wring our hands. Go, McCarter."

The crowds in Munzoga's city plaza had thinned out considerably. Encizo and Nemtala took one area, Salibogo and McCarter another. Katzenelenbogen, his skill with the Cairo dialect adequate, did a solo.

The sight of the slung AK-47s, the hard urgency in the eyes of the roving band of interrogators worked wonders on the natives. Even if the nighthawks knew nothing, they were quick to say as much.

It only took five or six minutes of their man-on-the-street questioning to convince themselves they were not going to get anywhere. Those who had heard rumor of the existence of insurgent groups in the city were vague. Perhaps there were such, but they could not attach a name or address to the alleged rabble-rousers.

Again frustration built.

As Phoenix Force regrouped in a disgruntled huddle to discuss their collective failure, a break materialized.

At first they did not notice the disfigured, dirty-faced urchin as he closed in on them, his twisted-stick crutch tapping on the brick cobbles.

He tugged on the sleeve of her baggy field jacket. "You're looking for the man who sells information?" he said in Arabic. "The man who watched you before, ran off to tell the others?"

Nemtala knelt before the boy, took his hands in hers. From the top, she instructed, her voice impressing him with the urgency of the situation. "Please, Dembo," she said. "Tell us that again."

The beggar did as he was told. And as the story unfolded, their heads spun. Light at the end of the tunnel, a chance to save Manning.

Dembo had been watching as Salibogo and the one-armed man had made inquiries before. A man known as Ashwar Fawzi had been observed skulking in the background while they talked. He had seen Fawzi, apparently a free-lance informer, steal into the night. He had not given the incident a second thought. Fawzi was always wheeling and dealing. It was no business of his. But when the group of strangers had appeared in the city plaza, all looking desperately agitated, a tie-in immediately registered in the streetwise kid's brain.

"You know where this Fawzi is?" Nemtala asked. "Can you lead us to him?"

Dembo nodded slowly. "Yes. You give me ride in wagon?"

A moment later, all reloaded into the Land Rover, Nemtala and the lad sitting next to McCarter in front, they were careering out of the square, boring into a dark, winding tunnel on its opposite side. Dembo chattered with delight, forgetting to provide directions through the snake-winding streets from time to time.

Five minutes later Demo cautioned, "We are coming near where Ashwar lives."

"Pull over, McCarter," Katz snapped. "We'll go the rest of the way on foot. No point in giving the swine advance warning."

This time they left the Land Rover unguarded and melted into the gloom, their feet making a soft shush-shush in the sand. When Dembo's missing leg slowed them, Katz said, "McCarter, can you carry him?"

McCarter swept the fragile bundle up. "Righto, Katz," he said. "Phew. The little bugger needs a bath in the worst way."

"Here," the boy whispered perhaps a thousand feet farther on. "There's where he lives."

"Let's hope that the bastard has called it a day," Katz said, sliding his Beretta from its holster.

From the humble appearance of the adobe structure, it was obvious Fawzi's sell-out career was not flourishing. It was small, squat, fronting directly on the street. There were no walls of any sort to impede their assault.

McCarter put Dembo down, motioned him out of range of any gunfire. "Cover me," he said, advancing boldly on the decrepit plank door. "I'll blow the fucker down."

He rapped softly on the door. "Ashwar?" he called in a hushed, confidential tone.

Shortly there was stir behind the door. "Go away," the drowsy voice said.

With a vengeful snarl McCarter slammed his massive shoulders into the flimsy barrier. It fell inward with a splintery crash. McCarter charged forward, his Browning Hi-Power at ready.

Fawzi never knew what hit him. One moment he was alone in his bed, congratulating himself on the easy money the night's industry had provided, the next he was cowering on the floor, a crew of menacing giants standing over him. What was happening here?

Then, as the woman, the old man, the crippled boy eased themselves into the dark cubicle. . . .

He knew. A chilling spasm of terror racked his body.

And yet—once a con, always a con. He attempted to bluff things out. "Hey," he said in pidgin English, "no need for rough stuff. We can talk this over, can't we? We make a deal, huh, buddy? What you say?"

Someone lighted a candle across the room. When Fawzi saw the barely suppressed rage in the intruders' eyes, he knew he was in big trouble. He made a feeble effort to slide farther away from his visitors, but a huge foot dropped over his wrist, pinned him to the floor. He whimpered, went limp.

"Please," the ferret-faced man tried again. "You hurting me. No rough stuff, hear? We can talk. . . ."

Fawzi was not prepared for the vicious attack by the raven-haired tigress with the AK-47. The rifle barrel slashed down without warning, dislodged teeth on the right side of his face, painted the inside of his brain with acetylene-torch brightness.

"We have no time for games," Nemtala hissed in Arabic, her face inches from his. "The American. Tell us where they have taken him." The rifle came up again, the butt poised over his thin, hooked nose. "Talk. Or I will kill you by inches."

Fawzi's head snapped up; he understood he was not dealing with amateurs. "Please, madam," he wailed, shielding his face with his hands. "No more. I'll talk. I'll tell you everything you want to know. Only promise you'll spare me. I am only a simple man, trying to make a living however I can. He is named Bihar Jibril. I am not associated with those people. Believe me, I beg you. . . ."

Five minutes later Fawzi, his hands bound behind him, was being pushed from his own front door, flung roughly into the Land Rover between Nemtala and the driver. Smiling back at the wan-faced Dembo, she said, "Watch carefully, my friend. Warn us immediately if he guides us wrong."

"Yes, mistress," Dembo replied, newfound respect and awe in his voice.

The ELF stronghold was caught up in a frantic flurry of activity. Two Eritrean hardmen were gathering records, preparing for momentary getaway. In a brightly lighted back room, another member of the terrorists was stationed at an elaborate shortwave radio, trying desperately to raise someone on Blackwell's end of the line. While in the main parlor, lighted only by candles, a more grisly diversion was in progress.

And though all the terrorists knew the American mercenary would never leave their lair alive, they still knew flight was mandatory. His friends would move heaven and earth to find their comrade, to avenge his death. Thus it was essential that they absent themselves from Munzoga—at least for a while. But first, the sport at hand.

Gary Manning was stark naked, hanging by his wrists, his arms pulled at rigid forty-five-degree angles by ropes that were strung to overhead rafters in the high-domed structure. The four men in the room had trussed his ankles as well; his feet were suspended eighteen inches from the floor.

Manning's face was puffy, bruised, one eye almost swollen shut. His lips were gashed; a steady trickle of blood meandered down his chin. Stoic to the last, he had not answered any of their questions; he had denied them even the satisfaction of an outcry as they had punched at his face, as they had taken turns slashing away at his midsection. The grunting explosions of breath at each new blow—that was all they got from him.

"You are being unnecessarily difficult," Bihar Jibril—a dedicated inquisitor, black, fat, pockmarked—wheezed in excellent, cultured English.

"You know we will get what we want before we are through with you, don't you?" He leered. "Our methods can get to be very ugly."

Manning opened his eyes a crack, regarded Jibril with cold contempt. Still he said nothing.

"Who are you?" the interrogator continued. "Who do you represent? Who sent you...the rest of your gang...to Sudan? Was it the CIA? Is this another United States intervention in our internal affairs? Did you actually believe you could succeed? A handful of men such as yours?"

Manning remained silent.

Bihar Jibril stepped forward, face distorted with rage, smashed the Canadian in the belly full force. Manning groaned, fought for breath, sagged.

"We have a thing we do with a lamp socket," the ELF topcock said, his words slurred. "It will prove detrimental to your sex life, however. Please, American, be reasonable. Talk. Do not make us resort to such animalistic devices."

He paused, waited for a reply. And when Manning's breath finally evened out and his eyes opened again: "Your name. The name of your organization? Your last chance, hero. Answer me."

"Fuck you." Manning's defiance was bought at great cost.

"As you wish, my friend." Jibril deliberately puffed his cigarette to a hot, glowing ember, advanced on his victim. "For starters, then. Be stubborn, if your choose. We can be just as stubborn. As you will soon see."

Manning could not stifle his coarse groan.

The three Phoenix Force members and Salibogo and Nemtala crowded in a last-minute huddle against a looming, mud-brick wall, their presence obscured to the ELF sentry by a heavy buttress. They had come the last mile on foot, unwilling to chance having the LR's noise provide a tip-off to the enemy.

All listened intently as Katzenelenbogen sketched the battle plan. A beloved comrade's life was at stake; there was no room for the slightest miscue. A single outcry from an adjoining residence could alert the terrorists within the ELF hideout, put Manning in deadly jeopardy.

Salibogo would go first, serve as decoy while Encizo maneuvered atop the wall. Once the sentry was dispatched, Rafael would drop inside, see to the stealthy opening of the gate. A rooftop recon then, once the group infiltration was made. After that? Play it by ear.

But first there was the matter of Ashwar Fawzi.

Katz sent a flickering glance to McCarter, who stood behind the rat-bait informer, a stone-hard hand clamped across his mouth. McCarter nodded, tightened his grip on him, dragged him backward twenty-five feet into the gloom. He shoved him roughly into a convenient cul-de-sac in the wall.

"It's okay?" the man bleated softly as the Briton slightly relaxed his hold. "You free me now? Please, buddy, we got deal...." His eyes were liquid with pleading terror.

They were the traitor-for-hire's last words. McCarter deftly shifted, clamped the crook of his arm around Fawzi's throat. With a whistling grunt, McCarter applied merciless pressure. The sell-out man fought desperately against the steely choke bar closing his throat. His eyes bulged; his legs sagged.

When he was sure the Arab was dead, McCarter flung him away with a grimace, as if he were contaminated. Goodbye, sewer-bloom, he thought. You'll never play Judas again.

Salibogo was primed and ready as McCarter felt his way back through the darkness. Encizo was already in place at the wall, his silenced Walther stuck in his belt. With a grunt, McCarter leaned, let Katzenelenbogen use his knee for balance beam. A moment later Encizo, breathing hard, was edging up to form the key element in the three-man tower.

They heard the rasping slide of his boots on the wall. Another grunt. The weight was lifted. Encizo was up. A muffled thump sounded as Katz hit the ground again. Overhead Rafael was already moving down the line, a shadowy, flitting cat. Yakov gave Salibogo the go signal.

They could hear him engaging the guard in conversation, playing the lost man to the hilt. The ELF lookout tried repeatedly to get him moving, but he was tenacious and kept up his stupid dialogue until he was sure Encizo was in place.

Because they knew what to listen for, they heard the faint cough of the silencer-equipped Beretta as Salibogo caught the terrorist by surprise, pumped two rounds into his chest. "Let's go," Katz whispered. They moved out.

By the time they covered the remaining two hundred feet to the ELF's front door, Encizo had dropped inside. The gate hung halfway open, and Salibogo was dragging the ventilated trooper inside the walls. The minute they were inside, the gate snicked shut.

All froze in swift visual assessment. Then, Encizo darted to the right. Seconds later they saw him slithering silently across the high dome, heading for a small cupola at its top, where a dim light flickered. Breaths were sucked in, held as he reached the top, stared intently inside the room below. They saw his face darken with anger.

Rafael's crisp whisper carried down. "He's here. We barely made it in time. *Those bastards*."

"How many?" Yakov asked.

"I see four working on Gary. Some motion in the back part of the house."

"Weapons?"

"Yeah. All on standby, though. They're having enough fun without them."

"Get down here, Rafael."

And when a puffing Encizo rejoined them, he reported. "They've got Gary strung up on ropes. They're torturing him. Going at him with cigarettes. Someone's rigging up some kind of an electric-cord gadget."

Nemtala's eyes nearly exploded in her face. She swayed where she stood, fought back a despairing outcry.

As Encizo finished with the description of the inner layout, Yakov took over. "A simple rush," he said tersely, his face anguished yet controlled, adrenaline pumping savagely. "No misses. They can't have Gary, understand?"

"Gotcha," McCarter muttered.

"Rafael, you and Salibogo crash the back door the minute you hear anything. Blow them away. We're going in shooting. Take them by surprise."

The war party separated. The soft crunch of sand, the creak of leather, the click of lock and bolt hung on the night air. Then there was utter stillness.

Yakov, poised at the door, placed his ear against the thick plank and heard muffled voices within. With painstaking care he touched the door handle, gasped with relief as he found it unlocked. Overconfident fools, he thought. Slow millimeter by slow millimeter he turned the knob. His heart kicked as the latch disengaged. The door slowly swung open.

After the all-enshrouding gloom outside, the light glowing at the end of the side vestibule seemed almost blinding. They filtered inside and began their critical advance upon the main room.

But at the last crucial moment, as they verged on swinging into the parlor, there was a blunder— Nemtala's AK-47 came in contact with a hanging plant holder and made a muted clang.

"Wakkif. Min inta?" The sharp voice sounded alarm.

Even as the trio crashed into the arched opening, the ELF hardboys were breaking for their weapons. They were a millisecond too slow on the uptake. Katz, Nemtala and McCarter slid into view, their weapons booming. The minidomed living room was suddenly turned into deafening, hammering bedlam.

In the back of the building the other terrorists sprang up and went for their weapons. They were just in the process of straightening up when the back door crashed down under Rafael and Salibogo's determined onslaught. The radioman, interrupted in midconversation, took Salibogo's five-round line across his chest and was flung backward. He died with his blood pumping in thick gouts all over his shattered equipment.

Encizo dumped a flock of 5.56mm bone-crushers into the cramped office, caught the terror goons cold. They collapsed like deflated balloons, rendered the top-secret files useless by flooding them with jetting pints of blood. They screamed, writhed amid the scattered papers.

In the parlor, it was no contest.

The man branding Manning's chest with a cigarette made a desperate dive for a P-38 that lay atop an ornate rosewood mosaic table. His fingers were inches from it when Nemtala's rifle spat hellfire, the rounds falling low, her trajectory deliberately circumspect to avoid hitting her lover. Jibril screamed as two slugs chewed into his upper thighs, turned him into a rolling, clawing basket case.

He quickly went still, sank into apparent shock.

Yakov put a silenced round of 9mm into the chest of the man at Manning's right. He saw him spin, go down like a sack of wet concrete.

McCarter had the best angle of all. The two ELF stooges on the left were in clear view. The Cockney kill machine put the Browning Hi-Power on full auto and sent thirteen rounds of 9mm parabellum booming into them. They died quickly.

Again an awesome, draining silence closed in; all stood in slumped, momentary paralysis.

There was time for full impact of the bizarre scene—a medieval torture chamber with Manning naked, spread-eagled on a rope cross, his face bloodied, his chest spangled with angry, dark welts—to fully register.

Encizo broke the silence. "All clear back here," he called, moving up along with Salibogo.

"Clear here," Katz replied, shaking himself from his trance, gratitude that they had arrived in time foremost in his thoughts.

By then Nemtala was putting down her weapon, racing for the room's far corner, where she began fighting the anchoring rope tied to a decorative pillar there. She would not endure the sight of her lover, hanging like trussed beef, one second longer.

"All down?" Encizo said, entering the room, grimacing as he assessed the full extent of Manning's wounds.

"All down," Yakov responded, moving to the other wall to undo the second rope.

In that moment of lull, defenses down, they were caught by surprise. With a fanatic, last-ditch charge, his preliminary movements hidden by a heavy couch, Bihar Jibril was on his feet. And though he knew he was doomed, he was still determined to take one of these infidels—preferably the accursed, silent hero—with him.

He lurched toward the helplessly staring Manning one of the long-bladed knives meant for their captive's final torture in his hand. He was halfway across the room before anyone's reflexes cut in.

The AK-47s swept up, then froze. Any shot at this

close range would take Manning, also. McCarter, Encizo threw themselves forward in a futile move to catch
the terrorist leader from behind.

A blurred figure flashed from out of nowhere as
Nemtala, first to see Jibril's lunge, came in from the
left. Her rifle out of reach also, she reacted on pure instinct. Flesh against flesh. "No," she shrilled. "No,
Gary!"

She flung herself on the man's back, closed one arm
around his neck. Weak, staggering from his wounds,
he was still more than a match for the fragile girl. He
viciously shook her off, tried for disemboweling stroke
at Manning. But in a last, desperate exertion, Nemtala
caught his arm and hung on like a rabid pit bull. The
savage charge, the downward thrust of the man's arm
authored the unexpected disaster.

The long razor-sharp blade swung back, the man's
wrist flexing in hundred-eighty-degree turn and the
knife slashed up into her diaphragm, penetrated her
heart. Nemtala hung in midair momentarily, her eyes
wide with a mixture of disbelief and regret. As she
spun and began to fall, she propelled herself forward,
hands reaching, straining to touch Manning.

"Gary," she choked a last time, dark streams of
blood pouring from her lips. "Oh, my darling. . . ."

She was dead before she hit the floor.

"Tala!" Manning howled. *"Tala! No! God,
no. . . ."*

By then McCarter and Rafael both had Jibril in their
grip. McCarter was bringing up the Browning when a
horrendous, throat-rupturing bellow erupted from
Manning.

"No!" he called, the command booming in the domed room. *"Leave him! He's mine, do you hear? Mine!"*

They did as they were told, savoring the way the terrorist hardman gasped, struggled, his eyes all but bulging from his head as Salibogo and Yakov finished cutting Manning down.

Manning did not look at Nemtala; he did not pause over the pitiful curl of her body. Instead he walked on wobbly legs directly toward her murderer. His lips were drawn back; his eyes burned.

The ELF headman cringed before the oncoming avenger.

"Hold him," Manning grated, his voice seething. "Hold him, the way he held me."

Groaning, his fists flashing like a human windmill, Manning thumped the enemy. Again and again his ham-sized hands rocked the Arab's head.

Even after Jibril was dead—his face turned into shapeless, unrecognizable raw meat—Manning continued to flail away at him, Manning's howls gradually turning into uncontrollable, wrenching sobs. He could barely stand by then.

Katzenelenbogen finally intervened. "Enough, Gary," he said in a firm voice. "Enough, my friend. She is avenged."

It was then that the warrior turned, moving like a short-circuited robot, and went to Nemtala.

He fell to his knees beside her, brushed her hair gently back from her forehead. He lifted Nemtala, arranged her in his arms, stared into her face for long, sad moments.

He rocked her silently, burying his face in the juncture of shoulder and throat. "Tala, Tala," he crooned in soft, ragged monotone.

The others stood apart, eyes averted, emotions beaten by the tragedy at hand. Salibogo quietly left the room, his heart again savagely torn, tears of sorrow running down his face.

13

"Damn you, Malwal," Jeremiah Blackwell raged, pounding his radioman on the back, "get that connection back. The first time we get some info, and you can't hold the signal. Don't just sit there, do something."

"I'm sorry, General," the communications officer said, quailing before the madman's fury, "but it's not our equipment. The radio in Munzoga has apparently been destroyed. Their operator was talking about the American commandos, relaying information as he got it. Suddenly there was noise, the sound of shooting. Then the transmitter went dead."

Blackwell frowned, his frustration nearing a boiling point, then he flung himself from the command car. He paced back and forth, his hands clamped behind his back, talking nonstop under his breath.

When the transmission from Bihar Jibril had first begun blasting from the command car's speaker, and he had grasped the critical importance of the message, he had brought the convoy to an immediate halt. Hanging over the speaker, his pulse hammering in his temples, Blackwell had not been able to believe his ears.

A four-man team? An old man and a young girl? Nosing around Munzoga, asking all the wrong kind of questions? They had wiped out the Americans' contact agent, but not before he had spilled his guts. Not good. Not good at all.

But when he heard about the captive, whom they were at that very minute in the process of torturing for additional information, he had been reassured. What in hell was this, he had wondered. A four-man swat team?

Again the chill had returned. Maybe Jibril had counted four mercs. But there had to be more; these were merely the advance party. There was no way that small a force could have taken out the squads he had sent out after that girl.

His eyes had narrowed. Could it be? That woman from Abu Darash? Had she hooked up with whoever was on his ass? The twinge of fear became more pronounced. Oh, Christ, he thought, if she ever gets me between a rock and a hard place.... He recalled the gory mess she had made of Major Ochogilo and his henchmen, and he had shivered.

It cannot be, he had assured himself. A one-in-a-million shot that the girl would connect with the merc force.

What the hell? Why worry? He would get the real story soon enough. As soon as Jibril and his boys coaxed the details from their hostage.

Blackwell stormed back to the command car, confronted Lieutenant Malwal. "Anything?" he spat.

"Nothing, General. Their radio is definitely out of commission."

The haunted-eyed black broke into a fresh stream of cursing. How much had the phantom army learned from their inside man? How vulnerable was he? How soon before they alerted the Sudanese government, and their troops were on the move? Air cover, AWACS from Egypt, the whole smear?

The CIA force? How long before they were breathing down his neck?

Blackwell's heart rolled over. His crusade to consolidate the black masses of Africa. Would it die aborning?

No, he vowed. He would show the arrogant white bastards. He would give them a fight they'd never forget. And in the end he would prevail. The Blood Doctor would prevail. The Aswan *would* go down.

Though they still had miles to cover before reaching the staging area, starting the missile into Egypt, it could be done. They had a decided time advantage on the American attack force. Somehow they could manage to slide by whatever President al-Nemery was calling an army these days.

All-out effort. That's what it would take.

And Blackwell was equal to that.

"Try to get DeRosa on the radio," he barked. "Keep trying until you raise him. Call me when you do. Maybe we're gonna need them Ethiopian soldiers after all."

Then he was racing up and down the convoy, winding his arm in universal crank-up signal. "Wind them up, you bastards," he roared, a frantic, paranoid edge to his voice. "Move out. Keep up, damn you. We're gonna roll like we never rolled before. Double-time, you hear? Double-time."

Five minutes later the string of seventeen vehicles was under way, lurching itself deeper into the Nubian desert.

14

Dawn was painting its first metallic luster on the edge of the world when the men of Phoenix Force finished burying Nemtala. They dug a deep grave, then piled a high cairn of rocks over it to keep desert scavengers from disturbing her body.

There were no words, no prayers.

All hearts ached, went out to Manning and to Salibogo, who had lost so much already. They agreed that the brief idyll with Nemtala had changed Manning. He would be hurting for many and many a day. He would need all the support his comrades could give him.

When Manning and Salibogo left the grave site, they busied themselves with the final pack-up routines.

Keio Ohara, withdrawn, sulking over being left behind at Munzoga, huddled in the Land Rover, put the ARC-51 portable field communicator through its paces. Though he was well versed in radio technology, this was the first time he had patched into the Defense Satellite Communication System. So he was careful in mental recovery of the info provided by April Rose, inserting the codes, punching in frequencies, getting proper synch on the high-speed scrambler the Stony Man electronics wizards had insisted upon.

Receiving from a small dish antenna Keio erected

atop the LR, the DSC's satellite would relay Katz's message via computerized / technology—intricate patch-ins that boggled even Keio's mind—transmit it to the National Security Agency in Washington. The final relay would slice ozone between there and Stony Man. Once the message had been received and unscrambled, the answer would start back in reverse order.

As it turned out, setup alone consumed the best part of an hour. Now, finally, the frequency was right, the scrambler-tape recorder rolling. Yakov's conversation would be compacted to a near-instantaneous burst of radioelectronic energy, transmitted from Sudan to Washington in the same form. Stony Man's reply would arrive in the Nubian desert in the same compressed blurt.

Yakov pressed the mike close to his lips, began his update on progress thus far. When he came to Ibrahim's blockbuster breakthrough regarding the missile involvement his voice became very agitated, the words pouring forth.

"We must have air recon to find that launch site," he said. "So get Grimaldi over here. Our window is narrowing rapidly. I estimate flashpoint within forty-eight to seventy-two hours. If we cannot take out the launch site, we need backup who can."

As he handed the mike back to Keio, the radio whiz said, "Give them ten minutes, Yakov." He began flipping switches, twisting dials, programming the receive-record mode.

Ten-point-six minutes later, an LCD meter flashed; the recept console automatically began to roll. As quickly as it began it turned off. "Is that it?" Yakov said.

"Yes," Keio replied. "The wonders of science."

When playback was ready, he clicked a braking switch, commenced the rollover. "Message received," came the clanky, echoing voice. "Report to be digested. Prepare for reply at 1200 hours EST this date. Out."

Katzenelenbogen sighed heavily, still upset over breaking silence, signaled for McCarter to start the LR. Keio moved into the back seat, fell beside Manning. The FAV was in tow again. Encizo and Salibogo were in the Unimog.

Even though it cost him considerable pain—his burns medicated, his chest bandaged—Manning still turned to steal a last glance at Nemtala's resting place. The command car lurched forward, headed toward Munzoga. Manning kept looking back until the misted rise between the two brooding buttes finally faded out of sight.

"What about our little buddy, Dembo?" McCarter finally asked.

Yakov smiled softly. "I'll always remember him. I have a stash here that will set him up for life. He'll probably own half of Munzoga next time we see him."

"Feisty bugger," McCarter chuckled. "I wouldn't doubt it for a sec, mate."

The Land Rover picked up speed. Manning stared straight ahead now, the bleak desolation in his eyes painful to see.

15

Thirty-six hours passed, and by pushing forward day and night, Phoenix Force managed to cover four hundred miles. Only a hundred miles remained between them and the Red Sea. Somewhere in that ever-narrowing corridor they would meet Jeremiah Blackwell.

Evidence that they were closing fast became more abundant with each passing hour. Blackwell, too, was moving at breakneck pace; it was apparent that he knew he was being pursued, that he was hellbound to achieve his mission, no matter what the cost.

Phoenix Force had found three abandoned vehicles—two Unimog personnel carriers and an antiquated WW II German halftrack—victims of the relentless heat and dust. Later they found a half dozen blacks, stripped of their uniforms, all shot in the back of the head. The men were deserters from Abu Darash or Al-Rashad—pitiful beggars who had been a mere five miles on their way when Blackwell's recovery squads had caught up with them, made bloody example of them.

Bivouac areas became more easily identifiable, the desert turned into a vast dumping ground. Again there was no attempt to police the area, to conceal their route.

Thus far the coordinates provided by Abdel Ibrahim had proved to be dead-on.

Another Unimog was discovered. And with it two unburied bodies. Black Cobra was moving even faster, was running out of fuel and water. If Phoenix could just engage them before they reached their rendezvous—where fresh supplies would be waiting—they would acquire decided leverage, inflict punishing losses. And stop the Black Cobra attack on Aswan cold.

Katz pushed them even harder, all hands—even a rapidly recuperating Manning—taking turns at the wheel, otherwise doping out whenever and wherever they could. Though they had bogged down twice, had lost six hours to a tricky Land Rover clutch adjustment by McCarter, they could still roll faster than Blackwell's men. Only two vehicles to keep pace instead of the fleet of disintegrating vehicles up ahead. Six men who were vastly more dedicated to the mission at hand than the two-hundred-fifty-odd pickups left in the renegade camp.

The terrain got rougher by the hour. In the past eight hours the elevation had risen sharply; they had to be traveling at two thousand feet now, which made for slightly cooler weather by day, but took savage toll on rolling stock. The strain of the rugged inclines, the zigzagging climbing of steep hillsides were raising hell with the rubber and with the transmissions of both vehicles.

More worrisome was the fact that there had been no sign of the air cover promised by Stony Man in subsequent transmissions. Launched from a U.S. carrier based in the Gulf of Aden, their attack would carry heat detection devices, rocket cannon and HMGs. Once activated, Grimaldi presumably at the controls, it would make mincemeat of Blackwell's ragged-ass army.

And though Mack Bolan's ace marauders resented having to call in outside firepower, they realized time was working against them.

Where in hell was that plane?

It was dusk of their fifteenth day in Africa, the mountains to the east looming, when they received the definitive signal they had been waiting for. In the distance, not more than three miles off, they saw a whitish gray smudge rising from the mountain coulees—the smoke of dozens of campfires.

The Black Cobras in bivouac. Within striking distance.

Hearts revved up. Adrenaline began punching its way through each man's system. Guts tightened in apprehension, natural byproduct of body and intellect facing stress, coming to grips with the realization that by tomorrow at this time each commando might well be buzzard bait.

Phoenix hunkered down in a well-concealed defile a mile farther on. Though the rest clamored for night action, Yakov Katzenelenbogen decreed bivouac of their own. Weapon maintainance, R&R. And though all knew there would be precious little sleeping done tonight, they realized that even fits and starts of sleep would make them much more efficient the next day.

The FAV was stripped down, reloaded; extra ammo, grenades, grenade launchers were rearranged for

quick access. Kevlar flak jackets were passed out
despite objecting groans from the team. Assault rifles,
the Mark-19, even one of the Goryonovs, personal
sidearms were field-stripped, put into peak operating
condition.

Also, quiet talk. Energy rations forced down. Restless sleep. Grim, private reflections. While, less than
two miles away. . . the enemy. . . .

AT 0430 HOURS, an eerie skrim of fog floating in the
wadis, the temperature standing at fifty degrees, they
moved out. Keio drove the fast attack vehicle. Salibogo and Manning rode shotgun. Yakov, Rafael and
McCarter fanned out ahead, ran point. The Uzi, the
Stoner and the AK-47 held at port, they loped carefully up the narrow camel trail that wound tortuously
up the mountain.

Fifty yards forward. A stop to wave the FAV forward. Another fifty yards.

First contact with Black Cobra outriders was made
fifteen minutes later. Waving the FAV to full stop, af-
fixing silencers to the Beretta, the Browning and the
Walther, Yakov went prone and began crawling forward toward the sentry outpost. On his left and right,
McCarter and Rafael followed suit.

There were four guards visible in a swale off to the
right of the road. It would have been clever ambush if
the soldiers, wearied by the long night of watching,
had not built a small fire. Two stood warming their
hands over the crackling flames, while two others slept
beside the firehole. None had his rifle at ready position.

As they slid closer the Phoenix trio paused more often, their advance limited to mere inches. Momentarily they lost sight of the enemy as they eased up a small dune and came within fifteen feet of the careless terrorists. As they poked their heads up cautiously, drew no glances, Yakov wordlessly pointed out a target to each man and indicated his own.

At the last possible second, one of the Black Cobras heard a sliver of sound behind him, whirled, saw the three guns pointing down at him. He opened his mouth to scream a warning. Yakov's Beretta coughed, sent nine mills slashing through his throat. Even as he was flung back, dead before he hit the ground, Rafael and McCarter eased their rounds into soft, unsuspecting flesh.

"Fish in a barrel," McCarter said, grimacing.

They kicked the bodies over, made sure there were no survivors. McCarter jogged back to wave the FAV up.

They then held a brief war conference. The enemy was within hailing distance; they must be supercareful from here on in. Katz and Encizo moved out to the left, while McCarter, paired with Manning, took the right flank.

They heard random sounds ahead and to the right, the mutter of voices. Encizo surprised one groggy Cobra as he came over a dune, in the process of unbuckling his trousers. He punched out his brain with single .380 slug.

When they reached high ground, stole furtive looks down into the main camp, their hearts sank. Blackwell had outfoxed them. His army was not clustered in one area. Bivouacked at platoon strength, they were scattered all over the landscape.

There were only about twenty troops in this section. Some were awake, loading equipment into the single Unimog that was visible, but mostly they slept helter-skelter across the sandy floor of the wadi. Smoke to the right, climbing from deeper recesses and kettles in the craggy hills, indicated numerous pockets of Black Cobras. If they hoped to surprise them, open up with withering fire screen from all sides, take them all at once—forget it.

"Shit-fire," Encizo muttered, "we gotta clean out one rat's nest at a time."

"And once we start," Yakov sighed, "we'll alert the rest. Two hundred fifty soldiers. Even with the Mark 19 the odds are impossible. Eventually they have to overrun us."

After a long, frowning pause, he sent Encizo after McCarter and Manning. "Tell them to recon the entire area. I'll take this end. Report back here as fast as you can."

By now the sky was beginning to take on first silver sheen; more and more troops were beginning to stir.

"Just like you said," Rafael reported as they regrouped perhaps ten minutes later. "They're in ten different groups. It'll be a hornets' nest the minute we open up."

Manning was even more troubled. "Something's screwy here. I count a hundred fifty, hundred sixty soldiers, maybe less."

"Strange," Katz said. "We were getting estimates all the way up to three hundred. Ibrahim gave me that figure, also. Deserters, maybe. But that many?''

"I don't like the looks of it,'' Manning persisted.

The Phoenix headman cast a wary eye skyward. "It'll be daybreak soon," he said. "We can't wait much longer. If we're going to surprise them at all, we had best be getting at it."

"Take them out one hole at a time?" Manning asked. "Use our silencers? Man to man?"

"Can't risk it," Yakov replied. "Someone raises an alarm, and we're caught without the tactical cover the MK-19 provides." He fell into deep thought.

They withdrew to where Keio and Salibogo waited in the FAV. Katzenelenbogen outlined a battle plan in which they would take out the first three pockets of Cobras in swift west-to-east with the motor mount, McCarter lobbing in 40mm grenade cartridges as fast as the Mark 19 could spit them out. Once the troops were thrown into demoralized panic, Phoenix would bore in, commence selective hunt-and-peck with its SMGs.

"Manning and I will take the first pocket." He pointed right. "Rafael, you and Salibogo take the middle one. By then McCarter should be working on the far left. We'll leapfrog you guys. Then you join in as soon as you can."

"What then?" Keio asked from behind the FAV's wheel.

"The main force will be scrambling by then," Yakov said. "We'll make for that hill over there." He indicated a high outcropping located to the right and deeper into enemy country, which was ringed with natural rock palisades at least thirty feet high.

"We make our stand there, nickel-and-dime them to death.

"Move on position, Rafael and Salibogo," Katz commanded. "Manning, this way. McCarter, when you see us hit the ground. Indiscriminate fire. Ten rounds. Then move on to the middle pothole." He regarded each with quick, proud glance. "Good luck, men."

Boots thudding a dull tattoo on the hardpan, each duo broke for the lip of its assigned witch's caldron. McCarter slanted up the Mark 19's barrel, slapped the cocking handle. "Reveille, you bastards," he muttered.

In the first swale the Black Cobras were caught totally off guard. The rain of 40mm cartridges came in faster than the human brain could count. The first explosive rounds hit rock or screwed into human flesh, detonating with ear-shattering impact, sending screaming shrapnel in all directions, trapping the terrorists.

The concussive effect of the minitorpedoes, the ripping hail of pellet-sized shards froze them where they stood or lay. They were caught in a deadly corn popper, maiming flesh-shredders coming at them from every direction. The eardrum-popping explosion at close hand was punishment enough, and some were killed by concussion alone. They stood in swaying, dazed pose, blood pouring from ears and mouths, from a hundred other gougings in their flesh.

Three rounds careered into a Unimog, reduced it to rubble, sent larger-sized shrapnel shrieking back into the screaming, milling terrorists. The fuel tanks went up with a muffled boom, spraying flaming diesel across the death arena.

A Cobra ran blindly back and forth, gaping, empty holes where his eyes once were. Screams rupturing his throat, he ran directly into a flaming river of fuel, fell and quickly turned into a human torch.

Across from him a comrade had taken a direct hit from a grenade cartridge. He disintegrated, pieces of his body flying in all directions, reduced to human garbage. Next to him, another Cobra, receiving spinoff effect of the blast, doggedly fought to stuff his guts back into place.

Those not killed outright by the swift, in-and-out bursts were methodically offed by Yakov and Manning, each man firing single shots at survivors.

When the platoon was eradicated, nothing left but shattered, charred corpses, a black cloud of smoke coiling savagely upward, Yakov and Manning sprang up and raced full tilt for the third battle area. As they ran they saw the FAV streaking ahead of them with unnerving, silent speed, the Mark 19 in full bay. To the right Encizo and Salibogo were determinedly finishing off their terrorist complement.

As they pounded up to the lip of the third hellhole, they heard the stutter of Kalashnikov assault rifles building deeper within the bivouac where the rest of the Cobras, jarred from sleep, hurried to get into the act. A Goryonov SG34 opened fire directly up front, the high-velocity rounds shrieking as they hurtled overhead.

McCarter paused in his close-quarter massacre, casually raised his trajectory, floated rounds at the

Johnny-come-latelies, at a Unimog that was growling furiously to achieve high ground. A cluster of forty mills dropped on the PC, and it suddenly humped high as its tanks exploded. The gunner was airborne, chopped into thirty different pieces. Head, arms, legs, streamers of human intestines drifted into the flaming desert skillet.

Abruptly, the effects of the Mark 19 stunning, everything went on hold. The main elements of Blackwell's force fell back—after seeing forty-six men wiped out—to plan a less decimating counterstrategy.

Yakov and Manning continued with the chores at hand. McCarter fired extra rounds. As Encizo and Salibogo came charging up, they were disengaging, darting for cover behind a long rocky ridge. Another diehard Cobra began spinning Russian lead in their direction.

Keio put the FAV into tricky dipsy-doodle, spun the vehicle out of range. McCarter, stretching for every inch of the Mark 19's sixteen-hundred-meter range, turned the hardmen into doggy-bits. Then he gave the MMG a rest.

"Fall back," Yakov bellowed. "Regroup according to plan."

Phoenix Force gained its preassigned rock pile, collapsed in gasping, sweaty sprawl. Shortly the FAV slid up behind them in noiseless tilt. They took turns rummaging its storage areas for fresh magazines. "My bloody ass," McCarter chortled as he dug out the humungous, fifty-pound, fifty-round MK-19 magazine, set it at his feet for easy reload, "if this gun ain't some piece of work. I'm a one-man army."

Gradually breaths evened out, battle tremors subsided. Glancing up, they were bemused to see that the sun was just coming up over the mountains. It seemed they had been fighting for hours.

The Black Cobra forces, thrown into critical disarray by the surprise attack, did not launch an attack for more than an hour.

Katz kept careful watch through Bausch and Lomb 10x50 binoculars and was able to predict the terrorist strategy almost before they put it in motion. And as he saw enemy action to the north and south of their position, as he saw Unimogs—with their Goryonovs—being moved into range, he said, "A pincer movement. That figures. The classic counter to that is a chop through before they close ranks."

Phoenix's field marshal relocated his troops, set up a new firebase in a stone stockade to the north, closer to the trail. From this highpoint they could observe the snaking road heading to the northeast where it wound for miles beneath them; under no circumstances was Blackwell to be allowed a back-door fade.

Their own Goryonov MMG was carried to the top of a forty-foot-high bluff, mounted in an impregnable nest and turned over to Manning. He would keep the enemy foot-sloggers honest, plus cover the FAV, as Keio and McCarter ripped the Cobra mousetrap to shreds wherever they could.

Finally, at 0730 hours, the pincer on verge of snapping shut, Katz gave Manning a brusque high sign. The Goryonov began punching out rounds, harvesting any human flesh found within its five-thousand-foot range.

At the same time Keio Ohara sent the FAV jack-rabbiting across the uneven terrain, heading for the southernmost extension of the closing circle. McCarter, hanging on to the Mark 19 for dear life, opened up with deadly, sweeping bursts that gave the Cobras in that sector definite second thoughts. Any round touching close meant instant death.

As Keio put the baby buggy to forty miles per hour and swung back along the front in zigzagging, bouncing flight, McCarter rotated the MMG, slapped rounds at the Unimogs, defiant challenge to the pesky Goryonov rounds snapping and whining in the air just five feet behind the FAV. One Unimog took cluster rounds and was turned into a booming fireball, its gunners reduced to bloody hash.

The other Cobras fell back. Still there was random AK-47 fire, which Keio negated with swift, swerving maneuvers.

But abruptly, as he rammed the FAV closer to the terrorist line, made a wide sweep to double back, the lanky Japanese grunted, keeled over, lost control of the steering wheel. McCarter fell back, grabbed it, wrenched the vehicle back into control from a nearly prone position.

As quickly a groggy, wincing Keio was fighting his way up, recapturing the wheel. "I got it. I'm okay."

"Where'd they get you?" McCarter said, back behind the MK-19, spraying grenade cartridges again.

"In the chest. It didn't penetrate the Kevlar, but it sure's hell gave me a punch. Couldn't get my breath for a second. Man, that hurts."

"Chipped a bone, do you think?"

"Could be." Keio gasped sharply. "There that's better."

Now they saw Yakov, Salibogo and Rafael hotfooting it across the terrain to their right, following the designated course. Again Keio whizzed the FAV into the corridor ahead of them, let McCarter bang pindown rounds into the prime attack zone. The Phoenix grunt party rose up from behind a rocky defilade, charged forward, dropped, charged forward in ragged sequence. A Kalashnikov opened up in tinny cacophony to the right, chipping stone at Yakov's feet. McCarter swung the Mark 19, hammered out four rounds.

No more opposition.

And as the trio went in for mop-up, Keio swung the FAV anew, took McCarter east, where the Brit once more raked the remaining Goryonovs and protected Phoenix's ass.

Up in his craggy aerie Manning did likewise, alternating between rearguard and front-line action.

Yakov, Rafael and Salibogo were going in. Definitive cleanup.

Ohara's lips curved in a snarl. He swerved the FAV and headed north. He and McCarter began chopping off another piece of the Cobra's tail.

In the pocket of Blackwell's hardmen Yakov and company found business on the slow side. Those terrorists who had not been wiped out immediately had cleared out and fled north to join the main contingent.

Out of the frying pan into the fire.

A Black Cobra hardnose, his face dripping with blood, staggered forward, determined to take some of the enemy with him. Encizo and Salibogo whirled just as he aimed for Katzenelenbogen. They pumped a dozen rounds into him, flung him high. When he came down his face was gone.

To the right, from a stony foxhole, another Cobra darted up, eyes glazed with hatred. Yakov stitched a four-round line across his chest, sent him to hell.

Again they moved right.

But here there was nothing left for them to do.

Suddenly as it had begun, there was an end to the battlefield clamor; an eerie silence swept across the stony plateau. In the distance they saw the Black Cobras in full retreat, heading deeper into the hills.

Overhead, Manning continued to pick stragglers off at will.

They were in process of turning, heading back for their own safe-house, when Yakov saw a blur of motion. There, amid a tangle of black uniforms, sidling from a minimound of gashed, pulverized black meat. . . .

"Get him," Yakov commanded, as the terrorist began running farther into the desert.

Salibogo brought up his AK-47. "No," Yakov roared. "Take him alive."

Salibogo's round screamed over the terrorist's head. Salibogo and Rafael broke into a mad dash and caught the fleeing Cobra a hundred feet farther on. From his vantage point Yakov could see the goon babbling in terror, pleading for his life. Rafael brought the terrorist back to Katz.

"Big troubles, Katz," the Cuban said as he gave the soldier a last vicious shove, dropped him at Katz's feet. "This ain't no African. He's Cuban. One of

Fidel's boys.'' He kicked the groveling man, who wore a single silver bar on his right shoulder. ''Tell him, *cabrón*.''

The blubbering officer stared pleadingly up at the Israeli, launched into a babble of Spanish, little of which Yakov understood.

''What is it?'' he snapped irritatedly. ''What's he saying?''

Encizo all but snarled the words. ''What he's saying is that we got the shit-end again. Blackwell's not here. He hasn't been since last night. He took two hundred of his best men. He's on his way to Aswan at this very minute.''

Katzenelenbogen's face fell. *''What?''*

''Manning was right. It *was* a decoy. These guys are ELF. Eritrean hardcases. Bought and sold like the whores they are.''

He loosed a volley of Spanish curses. ''A delaying action is what it was. And we bought it. Blackwell's suckered us, but good.''

Yakov's face was a study in enraged despair and frustration. For a long time he said nothing, the hooks of his prosthetic arm clicking furiously as they always did in stressful moments. His face was drawn when he finally looked up.

''That means he's got at least eighteen hours on us,'' he muttered, his voice ragged, barely audible in the wail of the desert wind.

16

McCarter, Katzenelenbogen, Manning and Salibogo were left to hold the high ground while Ohara and Encizo slogged back two miles to recover the Land Rover and the Unimog.

When the heavy-duty vehicles roared up, it was a matter of ten minutes before the FAV was reattached, the Goryonov hauled down, thrown into the Unimog. Twenty more rounds of 40mm grenade cartridges were lofted into the hills as a final hit against Blackwell's rear guard.

Phoenix was rumbling along the downside of Jebel Oda by 0900 hours.

On to Aswan.

The sullen crew jolted down the mountain. They all realized the long fuse—leading all the way to the High Dam itself—was already sputtering. For all they knew they were already too late; time was against them. Perhaps, no matter what they might do now, the Aswan was already doomed.

As they rocked down the spine-mangling excuse for a road, Yakov kept Keio on the radio. Stony Man must have an update, learn the mission's new, precarious status. Stony Man *must* provide intelligence on arrival time for the desperately needed air cover.

Where, in the remaining three hundred miles, would Blackwell establish his launch site? And how in hell—if it could be hidden anywhere from here to the High Dam—could Phoenix Force find it?

Keio handed Katz the microphone. There was considerably more vitriol in Yakov's report, in his demand for action, than he ordinarily might have used.

"Stony Three," the return transmission came ten minutes later. "Proceed with action to best of ability. Agent's arrival is imminent. Additional instructions to come."

And out.

The day droned on. Heat built up. Dust roiled and blew, clogged nostrils and throats, coated their faces in chalky stiffness. Still Yakov pushed McCarter harder, caused Encizo at the Unimog's wheel to shake his head in disbelief. Ten miles the first hour. Fifteen the second. Ten again. Then a stretch of plateau, transition between *jebel* and desert, where they made twenty.

At 0200 hours they came onto a long, barren expanse of desert plain. Keying on debris discarded by Blackwell's crew, they pushed on, the miniconvoy hitting an incredible pace of thirty-five.

IF YAKOV KATZENELENBOGEN WAS STEAMING, his anger was nothing compared to Jeremiah Blackwell's at that same moment. He had been waiting in a concealed wadi ten miles outside Halaib for three hours. Where was his missile? What was keeping them? Though presumably invested with more than enough lead time on his American pursuers, he was still edgy.

Then, when the missile finally came into view—still

in its forty-foot-long crate, flat on its disguised missile carrier—and Blackwell was informed by the Russian rocket technicians that the bastardized weapon had to be launched within a twenty-five-mile radius of the Aswan. . . .

His rage knew no bounds.

Had it come to this? Five million dollars, how many troops already slaughtered, his holy crusade? All going down the tube because some bumbling Ivan had chintzed at the last minute? Ajax Nike missiles. They had become nearly obsolete the day after they were introduced into the U.S. SAM arsenal in 1954.

And though the tech team assured him that the Ajax Nike was one hundred percent operative, that there was no way it could fail to destroy the Aswan, Blackwell felt it was a goddamned joke. A toy.

Two hundred miles of bad-assed terrain still stood between him and the High Dam. One hundred seventy miles if the twenty-five range was discounted.

In due course Blackwell's fury subsided. He was determined to succeed. Somebody gives you lemons, you make lemonade. It had been a lifelong motto. There was no reason the philosophy would not work now.

He had a jump on that CIA outfit, whoever they were. He knew where he was headed; they didn't.

The odds were still heavily weighted in his favor.

He gave his officers a tired grin, feigned more confidence than he felt. "Get them mothers mounted up," he commanded. "We got some miles to cover. Move 'em out."

Ten minutes later the abbreviated convoy (only

twelve vehicles now, fewer than two hundred troops)
began sluggish toiling into the Nubian desert.

They headed in a north-northwest direction.

They headed for thc Aswan High Dam.

THE TRAIL was easy enough for Phoenix to follow—
until they reached Halaib. At Halaib they found
enough litter to convince them that the scent was dcfi-
nitely hot. They had closed the gap; Blackwell was
only tcn or twelve hours ahead of them now.

But as they progressed deeper into the desert they
found that the Black Cobras had taken to cleaning up
their act. Now there was little or no throwaway, and
they were forced to rely on tire tracks, deep gouges left
by dig-outs. Even these were not to be counted on,
however; the eternal winds sweeping down from the
coastal highlands effectively obliterated most of them.

The missile itself left the most telling clue. Even with
the wind's dustover, there still remained faint depres-
sions—dug by the heavy carrier wheels—the next best
thing to a road sign.

Again Bolan's men turned into the walking dead.
The only sleep they got was while they were rolling.

As they crossed the Egyptian border they were
forced to abandon the Unimog because fuel was running short. It became expedient to consolidate supplies, keep the LR rolling. The decision was not made
without considerable complaining by Salibogo. To
leave that horde of beautiful Kalashnikov rifles and all
that ammo, he said, was sacrilege.

As concession to the old man, they wasted valuable
time rolling the PC deeper into the desert, ducking it

behind a low butte. Salibogo vowed that he would re-
locate the site some day and rescue the weapons.

Latest word from Stony Man assured them that
Jack Grimaldi was finally on the turf. He was supposed to be cruising overhead, at a superhigh altitude,
invisible to Blackwell's forces, at that very moment.
Grimaldi was to be using heat detection devices, radar
and recon optics. Contact frequencies were duly rattled off and noted by Keio Ohara.

But the desert heat, the nonstop buck and jolt of the
overland ride had taken its toll; thus far the Japanese
radio wizard had been unable to bring in Grimaldi.

If this was not crisis enough, Keio now found that
he could not receive satellite relays from Stony Man,
either. How, he fumed, could he know if Stony Man
was even receiving his transmissions? The whip aerial
was double-checked, the dish antenna as well, but
nothing was wrong. Cursing the fact that they could
not stop, and he had to attempt to rebuild while they
rolled, he was fit to be tied.

Phoenix Force had been on the move for thirty-three
hours, mostly nonstop, the only down time allowed being for pit stops and vital vehicle maintenance. There
were no meal breaks; they subsisted on energy bars
washed down with brackish water from their canteens.

Thus, at 1800 hours of that second day, as they
came over the top of a rugged rise, and Yakov called
an unexpected halt, all took it as an excuse for minor
celebration.

Their celebration was short-lived; Katz whipped the
binoculars to his face and scanned the landscape perhaps a mile and a half ahead.

"Is it Blackwell?" Encizo said, watching his boss. "You mean we've caught up with him already?"

"Can't tell," Yakov muttered. "But there's something out there. A lot of hanging dust, something that looks like smoke."

"Another false alarm," McCarter grumbled. "They settling in for the night?"

Katz raised an eyebrow. "Better than we think. The jackpot maybe. My calculations put us within twenty or thirty miles of Aswan. Lake Nasser is right over the mountains."

"Cocky bastard," Manning snorted. "Stupid bastard. If he doesn't observe more field security than that. He should take an ad on tv."

"He still thinks we're back in Sudan," Keio remarked.

"Good," said Yakov. "Let him keep thinking that." Directing McCarter to edge the Land Rover behind a fifty-foot dune, he got out and began swatting dust from his clothes. He buckled on his cartridge belt, reached for the Uzi. "Well, Manning and Rafael? Feel like taking a little walk?"

"Hey, Katz," McCarter protested. "Don't go leaving me behind."

"Dust off the Mark 19, McCarter. You and Salibogo get the FAV ready. Keio, keep at that radio. We'll be needing it before the night gets much older."

Moving out to the right, using the endless ranks of sand dunes for cover, the three men began moving west.

McCarter began running a swift field check on the supergun, checking the starting links on the sausage-sized cartridges that led up from the Mark 19's huge magazine.

It took Yakov, Rafael and Manning an hour to reach the outermost perimeters of the Black Cobra camp. By then dusk had fallen. Still, there was enough light for visual recon.

As they looked down into the deep, pitted ravine, they were awed. The area was apparently an abandoned mine, the terrain giving way to a great crater. Farther away, the land provided excellent cover for Blackwell's evil purposes. A hundred missiles could be set up with no one the wiser.

Encizo whistled softly. "What do you make of it, *compadre*?"

"Phosphate, probably," Katz replied. "The mine didn't pay off, and they abandoned it. Egypt's mineral poor."

"And we've got to flush the Cobras out of that maze?" Manning said, his heart sinking.

They watched in silence as the Black Cobra troops moved with obvious unconcern, preoccupied with their evening meal. Small fires pierced the gloom of the cavernous encampment.

"Is our friend, the Blood Doctor that sure of himself?" Rafael asked. "I could pot six of them from here. Yet I don't see a guard."

"I'd step carefully," Manning offered. "When there are no sentries, that means alternative security devices. The perimeter's mined, or I miss my bet." He tore up long strands of bunch grass from the area in which they hunkered. "Sit tight, I'll go check."

Then, wincing and hissing when his bandages

pulled, he slithered over the lip of the dune, oozed down the other side. He moved toward the firebase with deliberate care, holding a long strand of grass before him, a foot above the ground. Shortly he faded out of sight.

"Yes," he said, having crawled back after fifteen minutes. "Claymores all over the place. This is no bivouac, guys. The real McCoy. They don't want any unexpected visitors."

"The missile?" Yakov asked. "See any sign of it?"

"No. They must have it in one of the deepest pits. Probably setting it up, arming it right now. It's here, though."

"How do you know?"

"I saw the carrier tracks. No mistaking them."

The urgency was reborn within Katzenelenbogen. "We've got to infiltrate as soon as we can. Hit that rocket before it goes up."

The desert night was deepening. But still, aided by the star shine, by the glow of dozens of campfires, they continued to study the cuts and gullies below, the hardpacked crisscross of loading roads. They paid special attention to one haul area in particular, the one skirting the whole two-mile curve of the main section.

"I'd suggest diversion," Manning said levelly. "Infiltration against two hundred well-armed troops? Not with six men. We have to set up a smoke screen, then swat them when they're looking the other way."

"You're right," Katz said, sending a respectful smile at the Canadian. "What have you got in mind?"

"I figure if we can get the FAV up on that road, have McCarter and Keio open up with rifles, that will suck Blackwell's stooges in. They don't know about the Mark 19...or Keio's kiddy car...yet. When they move in, thinking to cut them up, McCarter will switch to Big Ben. Keio will keep whizzing up and down that road overhead. They'll never know what hit them.

"We, in the meantime, will circle in from the rear, attack from there. That way we'll get the main force in a matter of minutes."

"And the missile team?" Rafael challenged. "once they hear the commotion, they'll...."

"They'll crap," Manning finished for him. "What can they do? If the rocket's ready, it'll go off. If it isn't ready, there's not a damned thing they can do. Except eat it, maybe."

"I'm betting it isn't ready," Yakov said.

For five more minutes they remained prone, double-checking the network of roads, pinpointing pockets of greatest possible difficulty, establishing their own firebase.

As they started back: "Yakov? A favor?"

"Yes, Gary? What is it?"

"Tell the rest of them, will you.... If there's any possible way...that Blackwell bastard. He's mine, understand? Mine...."

17

Even in the swift-encroaching chill, Gary Manning was sweating bullets. Two antipersonnel mines to defuse before the FAV could pass, he was hovering over the first, a blade of grass floating around in a deadly cat-and-mouse struggle. He located a trip wire on each side of the charge and traced it back to the O-ring a millimeter at a time.

His fingers skated along the machined ridge of the striker housing until they found the empty firing-pin hole. His fingers slid up deftly, found the trigger arm, extended halfway down from the perpendicular. With a hissing intake of breath he eased the arm down and held it. His left hand snaked up, pulling a finishing nail from between his teeth. A click, and the mine was back on safety.

He moved to the right, following an eight-foot strand of monofilament. Again his fingers moved, the grass skated fleetingly. The slightest jar and....

"Through here, gang," he husked thirty seconds later. "All clear." He stacked the two claymores behind a rock to the left, then stood and waved Keio forward. The humming vehicle crunched past, Katz and Rafael walking slowly in front of it, indicating where the access road started.

There was hurried, last-minute briefing, as Yakov acquainted Keio and McCarter with the lay of the land. "We'll be circling around back there." He pointed. "No rounds farther than the third road, understand? Give us ten minutes to move in. Open up at 2020 hours exactly. When they start coming at you, go into phase two. Got it?"

"Ten-four," McCarter snapped, checking his watch. "Balls to the wall for them bloody bastards."

Then heads nodded, eyes met for last, swift reaffirmation of concern—and trust. Seconds later the FAV was sliding up the incline. Keio hugged the sheer inner wall to keep the Cobras from catching a glimpse of it.

"This way," Yakov urged, hitting low crouch, beginning a measured lope toward the length of the ditch closely skirting the main of the Black Cobra encampment. The sound of laughter, muttered conversations carried from less than twenty feet away as they infiltrated the chopped-up moonscape terrain.

Yakov, Rafael, Salibogo and Manning labored through the sand-rock clutter with deliberate movements, methodically testing each foothold before putting their weight down.

Breaths searing their throats, hearts hammering painfully in their chests, they paused at a crumbled opening in one interstice and took a long view of the main marshaling area. The vehicles were scattered, the Black Cobras hanging close to the fire. Some, oblivious to possible danger, confidently slept. The site resembled a stockyard, with its varied cutouts and separating walls.

It was a perfect place to use the MK-19. Animals penned for slaughter.

Manning climbed an incline, went on hands and knees again and made a cursory test for mines. Shortly he waved the others up. Yakov indicated that each man position himself at least one hundred feet apart. They waited, surprised that even though they knew where to look, they could not spot the FAV.

Which of these phosphorous-slagged cubicles contains our butcher friend, Blackwell, Katzenelenbogen mused. More importantly, where was the missile stashed? He strained for sight of distant glare, for something resembling a nose cone protruding from one of the pits. If the missile team was putting finishing touches on the liftoff, it would not be operating by firelight, that was certain.

Though decidedly dubious about the wisdom of his decision—the ARC-51 was still down; there had been no contact with Stony Man or Grimaldi in the past eight hours—Yakov was committed. What else could Phoenix Force do, with time slipping away on them so swiftly?

There was a flicker of motion overhead; Katz recognized McCarter, an AK-47 in his mitt. The Israeli sent a hasty high sigh to his flankers, then dropped behind a pile of rubble. The others followed his example.

Suddenly the night exploded. Two assault rifles opened up at full automatic from the forty-foot ledge overlooking the bivouac. Yakov saw seven terrorists fall in that first burst alone. He nodded silent encouragement as he noted how McCarter and Keio raced along the lip of the overhang, deliberately drawing fire, retreating, reappearing in another spot to give illusion of many troopers instead of just two.

The Black Cobras reacted coolly. Weapons were recovered, magazines slammed home. Hardcore mercs, they did not panic, but fell into position and began flanking left and right, closing on the high ground. AK-47s chattered in steady clamor, Russian lead screaming upward, punching into the solid rock face behind McCarter and Keio with potentially dangerous ricochet.

Yakov suppressed a smile as he saw how eagerly the Cobras hurried forward, arrogant in their intention to swat these pesky interlopers in swift frontal attack.

To the right, Katz saw the tall, cadaverous black, a ridiculously ornate dress cap on his head. The armed man decisively took charge, shouted orders, ran left in extreme sweep with a select cadre.

Katz glanced left and saw Manning watching Blackwell with rapt fascination. There's your man, Manning, he thought. And he would honor his comrade's request. Blackwell's execution would be in his hands alone.

By now the mine site was a crawling mass of humanity. And when the swarming was at its height. . . .

The FAV was suddenly darting along the rim of the roadway, the Mark 19 punching out its murderous, stunning charges in incredibly swift rangabang. Again the Israeli was amazed at the superpowerful shearing blast each HE shell set off, at the d-r-r-r-r-t stutter—in-and-out, leaving a dozen men reeling, falling, rolling, screaming in pain from the concussive effects alone.

Entire bodies came apart as if they had been stuffed with TNT. Clouds of blood, gristle, bone, bits of clothing exploded in a ten-foot radius.

Small wonder the majority of Blackwell's hardmen stood transfixed, staring, unable to react. Even had they had presence of mind to fire their Kalashnikovs, there was nothing to shoot at. The devil wagon was gone, streaking down the mountain trail, the monstrous gun spitting death into another area.

While behind them, before the faintest semblance of sanity returned, Manning, Encizo, Salibogo and Katzenelenbogen rose up as one and began filling their sector of the crater with flesh-shredders. Those who had not died during the thunder-fire overture checked out now.

Manning, his lips drawn back over his teeth, lost his battlefield smarts. Jamming three twenty-round mags in a row into the rifle, he fired wide open. One terrorist stood in stiff freeze, his finger locked on the trigger of his AK-47, spilling rounds heedlessly into the sky, his chest torn wide open, scraps of flesh flying like crimson confetti as Manning's slugs kept pouring in.

Then the ghost vehicle was skimming back again. The earth was erupting beneath their feet once more.

Encizo checkmated one particularly tenacious terrorist who—despite the fact that half of his face was a gaping, hanging flap of flesh and bone—was calmly leading the FAV with his rifle, waiting on a killing shot. What was left of his head was snapped back, where it hung in wobbling slack, the neck almost totally severed by the Cuban's last-minute burst.

Encizo began popping mercy rounds into three other still-flopping men in the slaughter pit.

Salibogo babbled an Arabic chant, gave his victims a traditional Koran send-off. Six Cobras fell before his clattering Kalashnikov.

By now the pits were dancing in flame. The Mark 19 scorchers chewed up Unimogs and random supply vehicles, spewed burning diesel into the night sky, set those hardmen unlucky enough to survive afire, turned them into screaming bundles of burning rags.

Little by little the sounds of rapid fire died down. Yakov and company now used judicious rounds—methodical extermination. McCarter and Ohara, holding the AK-47 and M-16 again, picked off those terrorists who had managed to take cover in select foxholes away from the main marshaling area.

Then it was into-the-valley time. Cleanup, the dirtiest part of any battle. Find Blackwell. Find that missile, chop it down before the night was minutes older.

Although the initial rat-shoot had consigned at least a hundred fifty Black Cobras to an eternal hell-slide, there were still forty-odd diehards at large on the outer peripheries of the battle zone, hardboys who clustered in pockets, caves and gullies, and were dedicated to fighting to the last.

Then there were some who had had quite enough for one night. A dozen or so of these Phoenix Force heard in the distance, as they stumbled over trip lines and were turned into flying dog-scraps, courtesy of the deadly claymores ringing their enclave.

"Ignorant bastards," McCarter growled as he looked down from his overhead vantage point. "Serves them right."

Movement to his right, a squad dashing closer to the base of his outlook, alerted McCarter. An ambush party setting in for a long vigil. He tried for an angle on them with his rifle, but there was no way he could get a shot without making a clay pigeon of himself. Abruptly he was up, running back to the fast attack vehicle.

"Live rounds," he howled as he returned and came to a stop above the spot where the four would-be bushwhackers were settling in. Three M-26 grenades, pins pulled in quick succession, homed in on the shallow gully.

His command carried clearly, and Phoenix's ground troops hit the dirt. The flat, concussive reports—BLAM-BLAM-BLAM—jarred them, rattled in echoing replay among the hills for ten seconds.

From the death-cage below McCarter and Keio came the sound of gurgling last breaths.

"Rotten, motherfucking bastards," Jeremiah Blackwell growled from an outlook located roughly two hundred feet south of where the pineapples had just bloomed. Blackwell grasped his badly bleeding left shoulder—a numbing shrapnel crease—and his panic rose.

He turned to the two men beside him, their glistening eyes reflecting the orange glow from the burning vehicles. "We gotta get to that missile, whip some Russian asses," he said. "*That bird's gotta go*. Once it does, we clear out. We get back to DeRosa, look us up a new stake. The mission worked, dammit. They can't turn us down now. C'mon, you poky shits, move."

McCarter and Ohara shouted overhead warnings,

pinpointed ground pockets and distant straggler movement as their comrades moved deeper into the canyon in search of the missile silo. Their rifles and the MK-19 ineffective now (the fleeing Cobras widening their range by the minute,) they followed the south-seeking scouts as far as they could on the stony ramp.

Now, as Yakov and the rest were finally lost in the eerie moonscape that seemed to stretch halfway to Sudan, they raced back toward the FAV.

Five minutes later they were entering the valley themselves. Keio driving, his M-16 across his lap, McCarter in half crouch beside him, the AK-47 panning. They dared any of Blackwell's diehards to take their chances.

They were two hundred yards into the mine floor, feeling their way along a main feeder road, when a Kalashnikov opened up to their right. "Down," McCarter bawled, instantly spotting the muzzle-flash. The Cobra was dug into a crevice some thirty feet along the pit's west face. He had been in the process of climbing up after the American death wagon. But now death had come looking for him.

McCarter slapped off six rounds of 5.56mm. The rounds did not faze the terrorist holdout. "We'll see about that," McCarter said. He swung up the Mark 19 and swatted three ear-splitting rounds toward the shielded hideout. In the blink of an eye the whole wall gave way, slammed down.

The FAV moved cautiously on.

It was Manning, exploring the extreme left flank, who heard the slight sound of a falling stone in a place where stone had been stable for a decade. He froze, sent a stand-off signal to Rafael, who followed behind and to the right. Manning eased to his knees, began a careful crawl forward.

He had covered eighteen feet and was just coming to the lip of the plateau, when he heard a muffled cough from below. He came to the edge, brought up his head inch-by-inch. There were three hardguys, in a boulder-hugging pose, all staring to their right, away from Manning.

The H&K slid into position, held bead on the man in the middle. Blackwell. Dear God, Manning thought, his heart hammering crazily, this is it.

"Freeze," he barked, the loud command jarring the three men, spinning them around. "Don't anybody move."

But the fools panicked; they would take a last shot at being heroes. The assault rifles swung up, fingers scrabbled for triggers. Manning pressured his own trigger and saw the guy on the left straighten up, spin into the rocks, his throat shattered. Simultaneously rounds from the right, from Blackwell, slid inches above his head, igniting a grating chill of mortality within Manning's brain. He dropped, rolled sideways.

Before he could take a stealthy peek, chance a second burst, Encizo had charged forward, hit the prone. The Stoner bellowed, the muzzle-flash illuminating the Cuban's snarling face, and the officer to Blackwell's right was sledged backward, taking four hard ones in the gut. The Stoner swung left and zeroed on the Black Cobra topcock as he flung himself over a low stone parapet, ran in zigzag crouch, heading deeper into the rubble of tracks, abandoned mining trolleys and slag.

"No," Manning yelled. "He's mine."

Encizo caught himself, slumped back. "Yeah, buddy," he sighed. "Go get the rat."

Two more shots cleaved the darkness, whistled wide and high. Blackwell's fireburst provided clear beacon for Manning. He saw the black maw of the tunnel almost at the same time that Blackwell did. And as the man broke for it, seeking to lose himself in its tangled depths, Manning sent a desperation grouping at the stone wall just above it.

The 7.62mm slugs hammered the soft shale, sent chips spattering back at Blackwell, momentarily blinding him. He ducked, threw his hands over his face, fought to clear his vision just long enough to still achieve his objective.

He was stumbling forward, his rifle out of action, groggily driving toward the cave, when Manning tackled him from behind.

Manning was standing over Blackwell, the H&K poised inches from his eyes, challenging him to wiggle, when Encizo, then Katzenelenbogen broke into view.

"The missile," Manning demanded, his voice emerging in a strange croak because of the overload of emotion in it. "Where is it?" The rifle barrel slashed, once, twice, across the sweat-glistening face, gouged out pieces of flesh. "Talk, damn you. Talk."

Quickly eyes became accustomed to the flickering half light. Seeing the cold, hateful stare Blackwell sent them, they felt a grudging sense of admiration for his cool control. "I ain't telling you motherfuckers nothing," he finally said. The words were dipped in venom.

But if his lips did not betray the missile's location, his eyes did. There was a furtive, sidelong twitch in them, a small veering to the right—indication that the silo was hidden farther on in the hellish maze of mining pits.

It was all the signal that Manning needed. His lust to avenge Nemtala throttled for too long now, the reality of having her tormentor now at hand, served to undermine any tenuous control.

"Manning," Katz called, his voice sharp, commanding, "stop."

"No!" Manning choked. The H&K came up again, began drifting across Blackwell's face, across his chest, across his belly, as if uncertain as to where to start shooting first.

The rifle came up again. It caressed Blackwell teasingly under the chin. "Do you remember that girl you abducted from Abu Darash?" Manning said in a hushed voice. "A girl named Nemtala?"

"Hey, man, who you shucking? I don't re—"

"The girl you raped?"

Blackwell jerked, his eyes darting wide. "Hey, you. . . ."

"The girl who killed your officers, then got away?" He paused to let his words sink in, the rifle continuing its mocking glide and nudge along the oily, black face. "Well, we found her. We helped her, nursed her back to life."

Again he paused. He grinned, savored the bewilderment in Blackwell's eyes as he moved a few paces away from him. "Here, you filthy bastard. . . . Regards from Abu Darash. Nemtala sends you this."

Blackwell's voice broke. *"No,"* he gasped. "Hey, man, you can't.... *No. Please, no* ...."

Manning hovered over the screaming man. "Was she good, Blackwell?" he mocked, his voice haunted, guttural. "Did you enjoy raping her? Was she worth all this?" The rifle roamed again. "Was she worth *this*?"

And he put four, deliberate rounds into his gut. BAM! BAM! BAM! BAM!

There is no accounting for the incredible ability of the human body to survive physical insult. For when, by all reasonable measure, Jeremiah Blackwell should have died on the spot, the body lingered. The body still thrashed. The throat still emitted grotesque animal squealings.

But not for long. Manning shot into his heart. Yakov and Rafael at last advanced and dared to pull Manning aside.

They stood beside him, bolstered him as he turned away and began to heave his guts out, the sound of his gagging somehow less loud than the wrenching sobs that now began, that threatened to rupture the lining of his throat.

As they held their comrade, stared bleakly across at each other, they understood once and for all how real was the thin line between love and hate.

18

Moments later, as Gary Manning finally regained composure, Katz caught a flitting motion in the corner of his eye and put the others instantly on guard.

But it was false alarm. Emerging silently from the gloom was McCarter.

"Taxi, anyone?" McCarter chuckled. "My last run tonight. Cheapest rates in town." A grinning Salibogo clung to the side of the FAV.

Seeing the grim expressions on the faces of his mates, noting Manning's withdrawn, slumped stance, he was concerned. "What happened? Did we miss something?"

Encizo sent a sidelong glance to the right but said nothing.

McCarter hopped from the FAV and was followed by a solicitous Salibogo as he slid down the slight incline. Both men stood silently over the mangled remains for a brief time. McCarter knew a spasm of queasiness.

"Blackwell?" McCarter asked.

Encizo nodded gravely.

"And that damned missile? You got that much out of him, didn't you?"

"I think we did," Katz answered. "It's up ahead.

Just where, I can't say.'' He climbed onto the FAV's running rail, clung to the rollover bars with his good arm. ''Move it.''

Again desperation built up as all realized that the technicians were now forewarned that the opposition was on the turf. If the missile was anywhere near lift-off, if the launch team was half as dedicated to the mission as Blackwell, they would be working frantically on last-minute calibrations, they would give their lives to make the bird fly.

Katz's eyes strained in the darkness for sight of any glimmer of light in the midst of these acres of phosphorous sores. Then, suddenly: ''Over there,'' he hissed. ''Did you see that?''

All eyes swept right, searched the inky blackness. As they came around a hundred-foot mound of slag, they detected a faint brightness against a rock face perhaps three-quarters of a mile deeper into the mine area.

Keio brought the FAV to ten, struggled valiantly to keep it on the badly deteriorated road.

''Close enough,'' Manning snapped as they came within five hundred yards of the base. He dropped off the vehicle, went in search of a blade of grass. ''Maybe they've mined here,'' he murmured. ''We can't afford to take any chances. McCarter, come along. I'll show you how this thing goes.''

Manning demonstrated how the Briton should fan the blade of grass across the terrain. ''The slightest resistance and you'll know you've got a customer.'' Manning produced a long wire probe; he began expert, delicate thrusts into the road's wheel ruts, the most logical place for buried mines.

They worked slowly, silently, moving ahead foot by foot, Keio sliding the FAV up each time Manning waved him on.

Tension built up maddeningly. More time lost. The missile could be in the act of being triggered at that very moment. As it turned out, there were no mines of any kind.

Finally Yakov ordered everyone off the vehicle. "We go in by foot from here. Keio, help Rafael lift off the Mark 19. The place will be crawling with Black Cobra guards. Blackwell isn't dumb enough. . .wasn't dumb enough. . .to leave the technicians on their own."

They followed Manning and McCarter in, skulking in low profile, feeling their way into the cleverly concealed site. Encizo shouldered the MK-19. Ohara labored under the magazines. Salibogo lugged the tripod.

As they found a trestled tunnel, saw bright light at its open end, they could understand why even McCarter and Keio, up on the hill, could not see it. The pit, reached by descending stagings where the Egyptians had worked until the mine petered out, was at least two hundred feet deep. There, in its deepest extension, was the missile, mounted on a steel gantry, pointed south at an eighty-degree angle.

Then, when Manning declared final all-clear, they eased forward and assumed stealthy station behind mounds of slag. They took a good look at the small rocket—only thirty-five, forty feet long at best.

"What in hell is it?" Keio murmured.

"Looks like a Nike Ajax to me," McCarter answered. On SAS duty in Laos and Vietnam in 1973, he had seen the missile before.

"Hell, aren't they damned near obsolete?" Encizo said.

"Don't sell that baby short," McCarter returned. "It's still used all over the world. If them techs know their stuff, the Nike Ajax will hit within ten square feet of the target. I'd expect it's carrying a one-megaton warhead. More than adequate. Once that baby hits, them old Egyptians can kiss their ass goodbye."

Katz was standing deep in shadow, his binoculars roving the site restlessly. "What do you see, Yakov?" Rafael asked.

"Much activity." The Phoenix headman smiled. "Looks as if we just might be in time. The Russians are going crazy down there putting finishing touches on things."

"Great," Encizo enthused. "We do get lucky sometimes."

Yakov beckoned for a strategy huddle; he outlined the part each man would play in the do-or-die rush of the launch site.

Each Phoenix Force member rose with grim determination in his eyes.

Shortly Rafael and Keio were picking their way down to the lower shelves, trying to work the Mark 19 to closer range, where its hell-dusters could do their ugly work. There were twenty Cobras and five technicians, Yakov had informed them. The MK-19 would provide surprise, soften-up barrage. The rest of the team, infiltrating to within fifty yards of the launching gantry, would concentrate on the rocket experts. No finger must be allowed to click that ignition switch.

Yakov, McCarter, Manning and Salibogo hugged the wall behind them and covered the duo as they crawled to the lip of shelf after shelf, carefully lowered themselves down, then lowered the minor cannon. They made four more shelves before they finally stopped. Drawing back into the shadows, they were seen no more.

Then the remaining marauders were scattering to circle the terrorists, beginning their grunting, sweating descent into hell.

It was tribute to the team's finely honed penetration skills that they were not observed as they slithered across mounds of overburden, as they utilized abandoned shafts, molded chameleonlike into open areas they were forced to traverse.

The Cobras were ready and waiting. Eyes darting, pondering the ominous silence off to the north, they watched for any sign of movement, for any betraying whisper of sound. Deeply entrenched in stonepile nests, three Goryonov MMGs in impregnable position—or so they thought—were deployed in a circling line some hundred yards from the missile. Anyone intending to abort their holy mission must come through them.

Black Africa's new dawn was in their hands. Blood Doctor was depending on them. They would not fail him.

Watching from above, Keio and Rafael caught a fleeting glimpse of their mates as they bored closer to the Cobra lines. They pinpointed the main nests, knew their fire must be true and swift. Without the FAV's mobility the Goryonovs would chop them to stew scraps once they achieved fix on the MK-19's position.

In and out. Get each foxhole with one quick burst.

Finally, there was no further movement by Phoenix Force.

"Here we go," Keio said, making a last check on the tripod, retesting the magazine lock.

Abruptly the terrorists were shaken from their fear stupor as the distant thunder started to the northwest. Unwisely they craned their necks, tried to see where the noise was coming from. In that split second the first grenade cartridges came floating in. There was an end-of-the-world detonation, a skull-collapsing explosion, a lethal sleet of lead. Tops of heads were suddenly missing; faces were turned to imploded mush; lungs ceased functioning.

In the first firehole the MMG operator never got off round one. And as those unlucky enough to survive leaped up to take over, there was ripping Uzi fire from directly in front of them; 9mm parabellums wrote bloody finish to lives that never amounted to a damn in the first place. Flesh chunked, bone splintered, blood gushed from a dozen different openings.

Fire station one became summarily inoperative.

Before the hardmen in the next foxhole were even able to get a handle on their desperate straits, the lightning-bolt weapon had switched direction, its trajectory was lifted. Again the fury bombs arced in. New bloodbath. Salibogo pumped AK-47 slugs into the flopping bundles of human flesh.

The murder monster moved on, to the extreme south, reaching for the circle's farthest arc. The death rain commenced anew, chewed away stone splinters with devastating force, compounded on the misery created by the splashing 40mm lead shards. It was Manning who emerged from the mist of smoke and blood, saw to a vengeful coup de grace.

McCarter, at the most distant lair of all—unreachable by the MK-19—cleaned out his complement singlehandedly. Using a trio of M-26 grenades for openers, his AK-47 to nail things down, he had five men ticketed for hell in seconds flat.

By this time, as ordered, Encizo was lobbing rounds to the rear of the Cobra lines, the Mark 19 straining to reach the base of the Nike Ajax missile itself, to chill the critical countdown if possible. The rounds kept falling short, and Rafael groaned with rage. The job was in the hands of the ground troops. He saw Yakov, Manning and Salibogo leaping toward the panicky technicians as they ducked for cover, streaked away from the gantry.

At that moment the ground trembled. A fiery, blinding ball of light—a million volts of incandescent fury—exploded at the base of the gantry. And with a jarring, throaty roar the Nike Ajax flung itself into the sky.

"No, goddammit, no," Encizo groaned, his hand shielding his eyes against the glare. Not now, he thought, not when we were so close.

McCarter saw the bird go, paused to pound three more slugs into a particularly stubborn terrorist, then he whirled back, his eyes following the white, jetting arrow as it climbed at eighty, a hundred, a hundred twenty miles per hour. His heart plummeted. "Goodbye, Aswan," he muttered in hoarse rage.

Those closest to the gantry swung back, caught the Soviet missile boys in the process of bringing up their own weapons. Yakov, Manning and Salibogo emptied their magazines into the half-ass warriors, garnered small satisfaction from watching their final death throes.

Then they froze into slumped, defeated stance, stared into the heavens.

The missile, a phosphorescent white hole, burned into the canopy of velvet sky, became smaller and smaller.

But then, with stunning, lung-compacting suddenness, the sky to the north seemed to open up, as if cleaved by a monstrous guillotine. And from that fissure, a new, deafening thunder.

Almost instantaneously there came the heart-stopping snarl of a jet, a mile up, its sonic boom splitting the firmament even as it closed on the Nike Ajax.

Grimaldi. The Tomcat. He had been there all the time, hanging back, heat sensors beamed precisely.

They could not see the Grumman F-14, nor could they see the Sidewinder AIM 9L that was now launched from underneath the Tomcat's wing. Almost simultaneously a second Sidewinder hissed into the night, backup should the initial rocket somehow fail to hit. It was upon the Nike Ajax before it was ten miles downrange.

There was a second sonic boom, a second jarring beneath their feet. The sky lighted up with a gigantic flash like heat lightning. The light illuminated the hard, victorious faces of the Phoenix team, cast harsh glare on the junk-pile chaos they had just created in the desert.

Somewhere over Lake Nasser stainless steel confetti rained down, like a Fourth of July flameout. The inactivated nuke warhead splashed down also and sank into two hundred feet of Nile water. Secretly dispatched U.S. Navy frogman teams would be weeks digging that baby out.

There were no cheers, no slapping on the back, no quick, congratulatory embraces. There was only a collective expulsion of breath, a rush of blood, an unspoken sense of pride.

Phoenix Force had come through again.

As might be expected, it was McCarter who summed up their feelings just then—with typical irreverence, to be sure.

"Grimaldi," he taunted the night sky, "you bloody bastard. Up there all the time, weren't you? Laughing your ass off at us. You'll never let us live this one down, will you?"

19

Saying goodbye to Salibogo Mugunga was one of the hardest things the men of Phoenix Force had ever had to do. In the fifteen days since their paths had crossed they had become as close as brothers. Insofar as one man could love another they had come to love the crusty old curmudgeon.

Fighting side by side, risking your life for one another will do that every time.

Jack Grimaldi, flying in at dawn behind the controls of a Sikorsky UH-60A Blackhawk, was standing by, the rotor-flap loud in the quiet desert air. All vital supplies, all components of their traveling armory were loaded. Only the laggard swat-team was holding up the program.

"C'mon, you guys," Grimaldi groused, "let's move it. Colonel Phoenix's waiting on you. What's with this old fart, anyway?"

They drew Salibogo apart, told him for the tenth time that it was impossible for them to take him along.

The Stony Man cleanup team, gathered from top-secret international sources, would arrive on the scene tomorrow. They would remove all evidence of this wholesale carnage from the face of the earth in a mat-

ter of days. The outside world must never know what
had transpired here, how close it had come to slipping
into the final abyss.

Apocalypse.

Salibogo was safe here until the cleanup crew arrived; he could salvage weapons, ammunition, supplies to his heart's content.

The Land Rover was his. Or he could take one of the
Unimogs that had miraculously survived the holo-
caust, Phoenix-style. And wasn't that what he wanted? To become Sudan's most successful arms dealer?
To be a wealthy man?

"No, effendi," Salibogo persisted, a heartbreaking
sadness in his eyes, "I no care about that. I want go
with you. We fight side by side again, no?"

"Maybe, my friend," Colonel Yakov Katzenelenbogen said, his voice—despite his years of hard
action—decidedly breaking just then. "Maybe, some-
day, somehow, we will fight together again. Who can
say? I hope so. You are a good soldier. A brave man.
We will all miss you."

Then it was time to go. One by one the Phoenix
team approached the old man, offered a firm hand-
clasp, a quick embrace. Encizo's Latin temperament
surfacing, he gave the weeping man a long bear hug.

"Hasta la vista," he said finally, blinking hard.
"Until we meet again, *abuelo*."

Manning, breaking with his traditional reserve, said
his farewells in the same way. And as they broke their
embrace, Salibogo looked up into his eyes, a plaintive,
shy smile twisting his battered face. "You not forget
Nemtala?"

"No, father," Manning said softly. "I will never forget Nemtala. For me she lives forever."

The old man stood just outside the rotor wash, his *galabieh* plastered to his scrawny body, waving feebly as they loaded aboard the Sikorsky. He forced a smile, but it was plain to all that his heart was not in it.

"Goodbye, Salibogo," McCarter called gruffly, fighting hard to retain his tough-guy image. "Don't you go standing at the wrong end of any camels, you hear?"

Then the hatch was dogged, the engines revved up. The copter—the FAV snugged on cables beneath—began slow lift-off.

For a long time after he could no longer see their faces, Salibogo stood in the desert, one arm still held high, but motionless. His heart leaden, he thought he would never see such fighting men—such friends—as they again.

In the chopper there were no words. All stared back at the lone figure in the desert. They watched as long as they could see him.

When they saw Salibogo move away, begin gathering weapons again, they all smiled. Some of the tightness in their throats was gone.

Gar Wilson is the pseudonym of a veteran antiterrorist expert who began his career with the Special Operations Group, Vietnam, in the mid-1960s. He later served with Delta Unit, a U.S. antiterrorist organization, and has worked with such international antiterrorist operations as Israel's Mossad, West Germany's GSG-9 and Britain's SAS. Owing to the policies of the United Nations and the U.S. government in the late 1970s, Wilson resigned his seat on the Coordinating Committee on Terrorism of the National Security Council. The author of the Phoenix Force series writes about antiterrorism in the manner he has always favored: expecting no quarter and giving none. His writing is renowned for its bloody realism.

MACK BOLAN

THE EXECUTIONER SERIES

I am not their judge, I am their judgment—I am their executioner.
                                        —*Mack Bolan,*
                                a.k.a. Col. John Phoenix

Mack Bolan is the free world's leading force in the new Terrorist Wars, defying all terrorists and destroying them piece by piece, using his Vietnam-trained tactics and knowledge of jungle warfare. Bolan's new war is the most exciting series ever to explode into print. You won't want to miss a single word. Start your collection now!

Available wherever paperbacks are sold.

GOLD EAGLE

HE'S EXPLOSIVE.
HE'S UNSTOPPABLE.
HE'S MACK BOLAN!

He learned his deadly skills in Vietnam...then put them to use by destroying the Mafia in a blazing one-man war. Now **Mack Bolan** is back to battle new threats to freedom. the enemies of justice and democracy—and he's recruited some high-powered combat teams to help. **Able Team**—Bolan's famous Death Squad, now reborn to tackle urban savagery too vicious for regular law enforcement. And **Phoenix Force**—five extraordinary warriors handpicked by Bolan to fight the dirtiest of anti-terrorist wars around the world.

Fight alongside these three courageous forces for freedom in all-new. pulse-pounding action-adventure novels! Travel to the jungles of South America. the scorching sands of the Sahara and the desolate mountains of Turkey. And feel the pressure and excitement building page after page. with nonstop action that keeps you enthralled until the explosive conclusion! Yes. Mack Bolan and his combat teams are living large...and they'll fight against all odds to protect our way of life!

Now you can have all the new Executioner novels delivered right to your home!

You won't want to miss a single one of these exciting new action-adventures. And you don't have to! Just fill out and mail the coupon following and we'll enter your name in the Executioner home subscription plan. You'll then receive four brand-new action-packed books in the Executioner series every other month. delivered right to your home! You'll get two **Mack Bolan** novels. one **Able Team** and one **Phoenix Force.** No need to worry about sellouts at the bookstore...you'll receive the latest books by mail as soon as they come off the presses. That's four enthralling action novels every other month. featuring all three of the exciting series included in The Executioner library. Mail the card today to start your adventure.

FREE! Mack Bolan bumper sticker.

When we receive your card we'll send your four explosive Executioner novels and. absolutely FREE, a Mack Bolan "Live Large" bumper sticker! This large. colorful bumper sticker will look great on your car. your bulletin board. or anywhere else you want people to know that you like to "Live Large." And you are under no obligation to buy anything—because your first four books come on a 10-day free trial! If you're not thrilled with these four exciting books. just return them to us and you'll owe nothing. The bumper sticker is yours to keep. FREE!

Don't miss a single one of these thrilling novels...mail the card now. while you're thinking about it. And get the Mack Bolan bumper sticker FREE!

BOLAN FIGHTS AGAINST ALL ODDS TO DEFEND FREEDOM

Mail this coupon today!